Joe's Bedtime Stories for Boys and Girls

Brian Harris

Illustrated by Children of Schools in Hertfordshire, UK.

authorHOUSE®

AuthorHouse™ UK Ltd.
500 Avebury Boulevard
Central Milton Keynes, MK9 2BE
www.authorhouse.co.uk
Phone: 08001974150

First published by AuthorHouse 8/27/2009

ISBN: 978-1-4389-7600-6 (sc)

This book is printed on acid-free paper.
www.joesbedtimestories.com
Email: joesbedtimestories@yahoo.com

Contents

Brian lives in Hertfordshire, England. He was a film technician and an award winning cameraman working on many well known movies. He now produces feature films. He is a member of the British Academy of Film and Television Arts (BAFTA) and was a technical advisor to The National Theatre.

e mail: joesbedtimestories@yahoo.com

This book is in memory of Leila and for my three beloved grandchildren; Joe, Luca and Annabelle.

KAIA SAVINO aged 8

JOE AND THE PICNIC

Once upon a time, in a land far, far away, lived a little boy called Joe. Joe lived with his Mummy and Daddy in a house in the country.

One day when all the world was warm and lovely, Joe decided that it would be a very good idea to have a picnic. He asked his Mummy to pack sandwiches, fruit and a large bottle of milk.

"Are you going to go alone?" asked Joe's Daddy.

"Oh no, I've asked some friends to come along," said Joe.

"Who have you asked?" said Mummy.

"Well let me see," said Joe. "There's my friend, Fred the Dragon, Sid the milkman, PC Luca and Annabelle."

"Where will you go for your picnic?" asked Daddy.

"There is a very big field at the bottom of our garden," said Joe, "and I think it is just the place to have a picnic."

"I just have to finish baking some bread for your school," said Joe's Mummy. "As soon as I have finished it, I'll make your sandwiches."

"Thank you, Mummy," said Joe.

Once Joe's Mummy made the bread, she and Daddy spent all morning making the sandwiches and Joe was starting to get impatient.

"I hope you finish soon," said Joe. "I'm getting very hungry."

"Nearly ready," said Mummy.

Just then, there was a ring at the door.

"I'll go," said Joe.

LACEY GIBSON aged 8

When he opened the door, Joe was very pleased to find that all his friends had arrived together.

"Hello, Joe," they all said.

"I hope you are as hungry as I am," said Joe, "because Mummy and Daddy have been making loads of sandwiches and we've got lots of milk to drink."

"I could eat a whole loaf of bread," said Fred, and everyone laughed because Fred, being a dragon, was big enough to carry out his promise.

Daddy brought all the sandwiches and milk to the door in a cool bag.

"Now be sure to eat it all up," he said to them all.

"We will," they all said together.

"I've got a big blanket for you to sit on," said Mummy.

"Thank you," they all said.

So the friends all walked to the bottom of the garden and out onto the green field.

"Where shall we spread the blanket?" asked PC Luca.

"Why not there, under the tree at the edge of the field?" said Joe.

Fred the Dragon laughed. "I know why!" he said. "After we've had our picnic you'll want to go to sleep and where better than under a tree?"

They all laughed together.

"Come on, let me have the blanket and I'll spread it out," said Annabelle, because she was very good at that sort of thing. She unfolded it, and a lovely gentle breeze blew underneath the blanket and helped spread it out. Joe sat down and opened the cool bag, but to his surprise, inside there was only a loaf of bread.

"Oh dear," said Joe. "I know what's happened: Mummy and Daddy have given the sandwiches to my school, and given me the loaf of bread by mistake. At least you can have that loaf of bread to eat!" Joe said to Fred the Dragon.

"But what shall we do?" said Sid the milkman.

"Why don't you all play a ball game, and I'll go to my school and get the sandwiches," said Joe.

"I'll come with you," said PC Luca, and off they went.

Sid the milkman had just finished the game with Fred the Dragon and Annabelle, when they heard the sound of a police car siren.

"Oh dear, what can that be?" asked Sid.

"I hope that there hasn't been an accident," said Fred.

They ran from the field back into Joe's garden and looked over the fence. But instead of an accident, they saw that PC Luca had arrived in his police car, not just with Joe, but with all of his friends from school as well.

Joe's friends were carrying bags of food and drink.

"Because Joe's Mummy had made such a lot of sandwiches, all his school friends have come along to eat them with us," said PC Luca.

Everybody ran into the field at the bottom of Joe's garden, and while Sid the milkman, PC Luca, Annabelle and Fred arranged all the sandwiches, Joe played games with all of his other friends.

"Come on. It's all ready to eat now," said Annabelle, pointing to the enormous spread of food.

So Joe and his friends sat down on the blanket, and they shared a magnificent picnic.

Once all the food had disappeared, Fred looked around for his friend Joe, but he was nowhere to be seen.

"I know where he will be," said PC Luca, getting out his magnifying glass, and Annabelle and Fred the Dragon followed PC Luca as he searched around the field for Joe. All of a sudden PC Luca said, "Aha, I've found him!" And there was Joe, curled up fast asleep under the tree at the side of the field.

"Would you like to come and play with us?" asked Fred to Joe, who had just woken up and was still a little bit sleepy.

"Yes please," said Joe, and they walked back to where all Joe's friends were waiting for him. They had a wonderful game and soon Joe's Mummy and Daddy arrived to tell them that all the other mummies and daddies had arrived too.

"I hope you've enjoyed yourselves," said Joe, and everyone agreed that it had been the best picnic they had ever been to.

And they all lived happily ever after.

ELLIE MANN aged 10

JOE AND ANNABELLE

Once upon a time, in a land far, far away, lived a little boy called Joe. Joe lived with his Mummy and Daddy in a house in the country.

One day, Joe asked his Mummy and Daddy if they would like to go for a walk to the shops.

"What are you going to buy there, Joe?" asked his Mummy.

"I need a new story book," said Joe.

As soon as they all had breakfast, off they went to the shops. They hadn't gone very far when they heard the sound of a big truck approaching.

"Now, who can that be making so much noise?" asked Daddy.

"I know," said Joe. "I've heard that sound so many times before: it's Annabelle in her truck!"

Sure enough, there just around the corner came Annabelle, zooming along in her truck. The moment she saw her friend Joe, she screeched to a halt.

"Good morning, Joe. Good morning," she said to Joe's Mummy and Daddy.

"Good morning to you, Annabelle," said Joe. "Where are you going to in such a hurry?"

"Well," said Annabelle, "I was sitting in my office, thinking that I had nothing to do today when the telephone rang, and it was this person saying he was very important. He asked me whether I could come over right away to talk about building a new house for him, and then do you know what happened?"

"No, what happened?" asked Joe.

EMMA LOUISE WATTS aged 10

"No sooner had I put down the telephone when it rang again, and it was Reginald Swan."

"What did he want?" asked Joe.

"He asked whether I could build him a play room!"

"But how are you going to manage to do all that work by yourself?" asked Daddy.

"It is rather a lot of work to do," said Annabelle.

"I've got a good idea," said Joe. "Why don't I help you do the building?"

"Would you really?" asked Annabelle. "That would be very helpful. Can Joe come with me?" she asked Joe's Mummy and Daddy.

"Of course he can," said Mummy," but be sure to be home in time for supper, won't you, Joe?"

"Of course I will," said Joe as he climbed aboard Annabelle's big truck.

"Where are we going first?" asked Joe.

"Let's go and see the very important person first, and find out exactly what sort of a house he wants."

"Good idea," said Joe.

Soon, Annabelle reached the edge of the town and came to a stop. She looked to the right and looked to the left.

"What are you doing?" asked Joe.

"Well, the very important person lives in a secret place, and only his very best friends are allowed to see where he lives. I'm just making sure that we are not being followed."

When Annabelle was certain that they were quite alone, she started off again. Soon they were out into the country and driving down a long road. At the end of the road was a big wall with a big gate in it. Annabelle stopped and pressed the buzzer at the side of the gate.

9

LUCY SHAW aged 10

"It's Annabelle," she said.

The gates started to open all by themselves, and Annabelle and Joe drove through.

They turned a corner and there in front of them were lots of trees. Annabelle stopped the truck!

"Why have you stopped?" asked Joe.

"You'll see!" said Annabelle.

Soon, they could hear a 'swish, swish, swish' sound, and to Joe's amazement, the very important person swooped down in his own private and very important looking yellow helicopter. The trouble was that its rotor blades made a huge cloud of dust as it landed.

"How good to see you, Joe and Annabelle," the very important person said, as he landed beside them. "Have you and Joe come to build my house, Annabelle?"

"Yes we have," said Annabelle, wiping the dust off her face.

"What sort of a house would you like?" Asked Joe.

I would like a big red and blue house," said the very important person. "How long will it take?" he asked Annabelle.

"I think it will take all day," said Annabelle. Then Annabelle saw Joe looking very worried.

"I think we have a problem, Annabelle."

"What's the problem Joe?" Annabelle asked.

"Well, if this person wants a new house and we still have to build a play room for Reginald Swan, how are we going to manage?"

"That's been worrying me too," said Annabelle. "Even with you helping me Joe, it is rather a lot of work. What do you think we should do?"

Joe thought for a long time and then looked up and smiled, because he had had a brilliant idea.

"Why don't we ask PC Luca to help? That way we can finish the very important person's house in the morning and go to Reginald Swan's house after lunch."

"You're so clever, Joe," said Annabelle. "But why are you still looking so worried?"

"I forgot that the very important person needs to keep his place secret and we won't be able to tell PC Luca where he lives."

"I'm sure it will be all right to tell PC Luca: after all, he is a policeman," said Annabelle.

So Joe called his friend, PC Luca, and soon they heard the sound of a police siren.

"What is that noise?" asked the very important person.

"That's my friend, PC Luca," said Joe, "and he has come to help build your house with me and Annabelle. That way, we will be able to finish it in time; and don't worry, he is a policeman and he will not tell anyone where you live."

PC Luca got out of his police car and put on his special overalls.

"Where do we start?" he asked.

We have to ask Annabelle, because that is what she is good at," said Joe.

"Let's begin at the bottom and build a ground floor, an upstairs and a roof," said Annabelle.

"What shall I do?" asked the very important person.

"Why not make a pot of tea?" suggested Joe.

While the very important person went off to make the tea, Joe and

Annabelle and PC Luca worked very hard, hammering, banging and building. By the time their tea was ready, Joe and his friends had built the whole downstairs of the house.

"Do you need anywhere special to keep your very important things?" Asked Joe.

"How clever of you to ask," said the very important person. "Yes please, I need somewhere to keep my yellow helicopter that I use for all my adventures."

"We'll put that in a special garage called a hangar and build it at the bottom of your garden so that when you fly in and out you won't blow all the dust from the rotor into the house," said Annabelle.

Soon Joe, Annabelle and PC Luca had finished the house and also the hangar at the bottom of the garden. The very important person asked if they would like to stay for lunch.

"We had better not," said Joe, "we have still got a play room to build for Reginald Swan."

"All I can say is that this is the best house I have ever seen. It has a red roof and blue bricks just as I wanted. Thank you all very much, especially you, Joe; if you hadn't have had such a good idea I would not have had my house built so quickly," said the very important person.

The three friends waved goodbye and drove off to see Reginald Swan.

They hadn't gone very far when they saw lots of birds in the sky.

"What are all those birds?" asked Annabelle.

"Just a minute I shall have a look," said PC Luca, getting out his magnifying glass.

"I know what they are," said Joe. "They are swans, so we must be getting very close to Reginald Swan's house!"

They turned a corner, and there was Reginald Swan's house with Reginald Swan standing outside.

"I'm really pleased to see you," said Reginald Swan. "Have you come to build my play room?"

"Yes we have," said Annabelle. "If we start now, we can be finished in one hour's time."

"What sort of play room would you like to have?" asked Annabelle.

"I want a big play room to keep all my toys," said Reginald Swan.

"Leave it to us," said Joe.

"Perhaps you would make us a jug of cool lemonade while we do our work?" Said PC Luca.

"I will," said Reginald Swan. They all thanked him as he flew off to make their drink.

By the time he returned, Annabelle, Joe and PC Luca had finished.

"What games would you like in your play room?" asked Joe.

"I would like Snakes and Ladders, some musical instruments, an ABC book and Snap," said Reginald Swan.

Joe placed everything Reginald Swan wanted in the play room.

The three friend said goodbye to Reginald Swan.

"I don't know about you," said Annabelle, "but because we worked all day long I've just remembered the one thing we have not done."

"What is that, Annabelle?" PC Luca asked.

"We have not had anything to eat, and I'm very hungry!"

Joe smiled; he had the answer. "My Mummy asked me to be home in time for supper; why don't you and PC Luca come back to my house, and we can all have supper together."

The three friends had a lovely supper at Joe's house, and by the time they finished, they all agreed that they had had a very busy day indeed.

And they all lived happily ever after.

COURTNEY PALMER aged 8

JOE AND FRED THE DRAGON

Once upon a time, in a land far, far away, lived a little boy called Joe. Joe lived with his Mummy and Daddy in a house in the country.

One day, Joe had a telephone call from his friend, Fred the Dragon.

"Are you going to school today, Joe?" asked Fred.

"Yes, but only for half a day. Would you like to play with me when I come home, Fred?"

"Yes I would," said Fred.

Just then, Joe's Mummy and Daddy came into the room. "Can Fred come to play with me this afternoon please?" asked Joe.

"Why not invite him for lunch?" said Joe's Mummy.

So Joe asked Fred to come for lunch.

"I'll be over at one o'clock," Fred said.

Joe went to school in the morning, and when his Daddy came to collect him he asked if Fred had arrived yet.

"Not yet," said Daddy.

When Joe arrived home he asked his Mummy, "Has Fred arrived yet?"

"Not yet," said his Mummy.

Soon it was lunch time, and Joe was very worried: he had not heard from his friend.

"I'll call Fred's Mummy and Daddy and see where he has got to," said Joe's Daddy.

ANANYA MUDERA aged 9

"I'll go outside to the lane and wait for him," said Joe.

He hadn't been waiting long, when Annabelle drove up in her truck. When Joe explained why he was waiting there, Annabelle asked if Fred would normally come down the lane.

"He was actually going to fly," said Joe.

"What, in an aeroplane?" asked Annabelle.

"No. You are silly Annabelle, Fred is a dragon, and he can fly all by himself," said Joe.

Annabelle laughed. "Oh of course, I forgot that dragons can fly," she said.

"As Fred is missing, would you like me to drive you to his house in Dragonland and see if we can find out where he might have gone?" asked Annabelle.

"Yes please," said Joe.

Off they drove in Annabelle's truck. They had not gone very far when they met PC Luca, standing by his police car that had broken down. When Joe told him where they were going, PC Luca thought he had better come along too.

"After all," he said, "it's a missing person, so sounds very like police business."

Both Annabelle and Joe nodded, and PC Luca climbed aboard Annabelle's truck, and off they all went.

As they got nearer and nearer to Dragonland where Fred's house was, the ground started to shake! Then a great noise was heard. PC Luca and Annabelle looked very worried because the noise was frightening them, but Joe started to laugh.

"Why are you laughing?" asked PC Luca.

"Because I now know where Fred is," said Joe.

"Where is he?" asked Annabelle, stopping her truck.

The ground still shook and the noise changed to a roar.

"Come with me," said Joe as he got out of the truck. Annabelle and PC Luca both followed him looking very puzzled, wondering why Joe was still laughing.

Soon they came to a wood, and the ground started to shake even more, and the sound grew into a mighty roar. PC Luca and Annabelle were very frightened! The more frightened they became, the more Joe laughed. They walked through the wood, and suddenly Joe stood still and pointed.

There under a tree was his friend, Fred the Dragon, and he was fast asleep. As he snored the ground shook, and the sound of his snoring rumbled through the wood.

The three friends laughed so much that they woke Fred from his very deep sleep.

"Hello," said Fred, rubbing his eyes.

"Hello Fred," said Joe. "We were very worried because you didn't come to play at one o'clock."

Fred looked at the time on his watch. He turned to Joe and said, "I'm so sorry

Joe; you see I worked so hard in school this morning that I grew very sleepy and had to have a lie down under this tree."

Joe laughed. "But that's what I do when I am sleepy," he said.

"I know, that's where I got the idea from," laughed Fred.

Once Fred had properly woken up, they all decided to drive the rest of the way to Joe's house in Annabelle's truck.

"What shall we do about my police car that has broken down?" asked PC Luca.

"I know," said Joe, "I'll call Dan the mechanic and ask if he can mend it by the time we get back to your car."

"Thank you Joe," said PC Luca, and sure enough, by the time they had driven back to PC Luca's car, Dan had mended the police car, and they were able to drive it to Joe's house. As soon as they all arrived, Joe's Mummy and Daddy telephoned Fred the Dragon's Mummy and Daddy to let them know that Fred was safe and well.

Then Joe's Mummy and Daddy agreed that it was now far too late to have lunch, and made a fabulous tea for everybody instead.

And they all lived happily ever after.

JOE AND THE SPOOKY MAZE

Once upon a time, in a land far, far away, lived a little boy called Joe. Joe lived with his Mummy and Daddy in a house in the country.

One day when Joe woke up, he saw that there was a letter for him from his friend William the Wizard. William asked if Joe could come right away and meet him outside the maze at Lavender Farm, to help him with a problem.

After breakfast, Joe quickly got dressed, and went to Lavender Farm to meet William. When he arrived at the farm there was no one there. Joe walked down to where he knew the maze was, but there was no sign of William.

"I wonder what I should do," thought Joe.

He was just about to enter the maze when he heard a noise. Joe looked around, and there was Louise the Tractor.

"Why, Joe, what are you doing here?" asked Louise.

"I had a letter from William the Wizard asking to meet me by the maze, but he is not here," said Joe.

"So what are you going to do?" asked Louise.

"I'm going into the maze to look for him," said Joe.

"You can't go in there," said Louise.

"Why ever not?" asked Joe.

"Don't you know that we call it the Spooky Maze," said Louise, "and a wicked ogre lives there? People have gone in there and have never been seen again."

"They have?" Joe asked. "Do you think that is where my friend, William the Wizard is?"

"All I can say," said Louise, "is that I'm not brave enough. I wouldn't go into the Spooky Maze if I were you."

"Well," said Joe, "I've got to find him, so I have to go."

"You're really brave, Joe," said Louise. "Good luck!"

Louise then drove off to the other side of the farm, leaving Joe standing all alone at the entrance to the Spooky Maze.

"Here I go," said Joe to no one in particular. He placed one foot inside the maze. When nothing happened he placed his other foot inside the maze.

"Just as I thought: nothing has happened yet," he said to himself.

Just then there was a crash of thunder, and the sky went very dark.

"Oh dear, I think it's going to rain," said Joe.

"Have you got an umbrella?" asked a small, squeaky voice.

There, flying just in front of his nose was a tiny little Fairy.

"No, I haven't got an umbrella," said Joe.

"Neither have I," said the Fairy.

"So why did you ask me?" asked Joe.

"Just making conversation," said the Fairy.

Just then it started to rain.

"Let's shelter over there," said the Fairy, pointing to a tiny house.

"It's far too small for me to get into," said Joe.

"Don't you worry about that," said the Fairy. She waved her magic wand.

There was a flash, followed by a bang, and Joe found himself shrinking down to the size of the Fairy.

The two of them opened the front door of the house, and went inside.

"I didn't know there were any houses in the maze," said Joe.

"You mean, the Spooky Maze," said the Fairy.

MANAV BABAR aged 9

"Is it really called that?" asked Joe.

"Strange things happen here," said the Fairy. She looked outside. "The rain has stopped," she said. "Why are you here, anyway?"

"I'm looking for my friend, William the Wizard," Joe said.

"If William is your friend, then you are a friend of mine. I would like to help you look for him!"

"Thank you," said Joe. "By the way, my name is Joe." Joe held out his hand, and the Fairy shook it.

"My name is Anastasia," she said. "How do you do?"

"Where shall we start to look for William?" asked Joe.

"The last time I saw him he was right in the centre of the maze," said Anastasia. "I'll take you there now," she said.

The two new friends left the little house. Just as they turned the corner the ground started to shake. Joe looked up, and was surprised to see an enormous ant.

"Wow, look at that!" he said to Anastasia. "That ant must be tall enough to reach the sky!"

"Quickly hide behind this tree," said Anastasia and the two ducked behind a tree as the monster ant walked by with the ground shaking all about him.

As soon as the monstrous ant was out of sight, fairy Anastasia took Joe's hand.

"Come on," she said, pulling Joe along the path.

They hadn't gone very far when the ground shook again, and this time the biggest beetle that Joe had ever seen walked passed.

"Wow!" said Joe. "Look at the size of that beetle!"

Then Joe stood still, and laughed and laughed. "Of course," he said, "you made me as tiny as you, and now all the insects are as big as monsters. Can you change me back please?" he asked Anastasia.

Anastasia waved her little Fairy wand. In a crash and a flash Joe was back to his real size, and the beetle looked tiny again.

"Thank you, Anastasia," he said.

"We are near the middle of the Spooky Maze," said Anastasia. "I think we should be very quiet now, so that we don't disturb the wicked ogre who lives there."

"But I thought you said that my friend, William the Wizard was there," said Joe.

"Yes, he was there, and he was watching the ogre. That must have been why he wrote a letter to you," said Anastasia. "You see, the ogre has been getting nastier and nastier, and he has been giving all of us who live here a horrible time."

"Where do you think William is now?" asked Joe.

"I think he may have been captured by the ogre," she said. "Hold my hand and we can go and look. Come on!"

Joe held the Fairy's tiny hand, and was surprised when they started to fly over the trees. Soon they came to a castle.

"Here we are: this is the very centre," said Anastasia. "Let's look in through that castle window over there."

Joe and the Fairy looked through the window. In the middle of the room was Joe's friend, William the Wizard. Poor William was tied to a chair, and could not move. Opposite him was a horrible ogre, eating his supper and laughing at William.

"When I finish my plate full of food, I think I will eat you too!" he said.

"What shall we do?" asked fairy Anastasia, looking at Joe.

Joe looked down at a spider that was making its way back to his web.

"You know how you made me as small as you?" Joe asked. "Can you make that spider as big as us?"

"Of course I can," said Anastasia. She waved her wand and with a crash and a flash the spider was made as big as a house.

"Now, Mr Spider," said Joe, "can you go into the castle and spin a web around the ogre?"

"I certainly can," said the spider.

He walked up the wall and, the now huge monster spider, crawled through the window.

"What do you mean by coming in through my window?" asked the horrible ogre. But before he could do anything, the spider wound an enormous web around the ogre. Fairy Anastasia held Joe's hand, and they flew through the window and rescued William the Wizard.

"Well done Joe, and thank you Anastasia," said William.

"What shall we do with him?" asked Joe, pointing to the ogre who was wrapped up in an enormous spider's web.

"Can I borrow your magic wand please, Anastasia?" Asked William.

Fairy Anastasia passed William her tiny wand.

"Abracadabra," said William, and the spider went back to his proper size and the ogre disappeared.

"Now that the ogre has gone," said Joe, "who should live in the castle?"

"I'm going to give it to all the fairies to live in, and then the maze will not be spooky anymore," said William.

"Can you ask all the fairies to come now?" William asked Anastasia.

"Of course," said Fairy Anastasia, and she waved her wand. As quick as a flash, all the fairies living in the maze arrived at the castle.

When they saw that the horrible ogre was no longer there, they all agreed to have a party.

When the party ended, everyone thanked Joe and fairy Anastasia for rescuing William the Wizard, and giving them such a wonderful new home.

William stood up and took a deep breath, and said at the top of his voice, "Now that there is no ogre, from now on this maze will be known as the Lavender Farm Maze, and as a reward for his bravery, Joe will always be able to ride on Louise the tractor's trailer whenever he wants."

Everyone patted Joe on the back, and they all sang, "for he's a jolly good fellow."

And they all lived happily ever after.

KAYLEIGH MILLAR aged 9

JOE AND THE GRAND OLD DUKE OF YORK

Once upon a time, in a land far, far away, lived a little boy called Joe. Joe lived with his Mummy and Daddy in a house in the country.

One day, Joe was walking in the country when he heard a noise down by the river. There was Mr and Mrs Duck arguing with Mr Brown, who was digging on the river bank.

"Whatever is the matter?" asked Joe.

"Mr Brown has to tidy up the river bank, but he is putting all the mud that he digs up into our front garden," said Mrs Duck. "I can't keep it clean for all my little family."

"Isn't there anywhere else you can put all that earth, Mr Brown?" asked Joe.

"It's very difficult to find places to put it, Joe. I'm very sorry, Mrs Duck, I'll try to be more careful, but I have to dig up all the earth before it falls into the river."

"Why not use a wheel barrow and take the mud further along the path?" asked Joe.

"I'll certainly try," said Mr Brown.

"Oh thank you, Joe," said Mrs Duck. "Won't you come in and have something to drink, and a lovely new duck egg with bread and butter?" She asked.

"That's very kind of you Mrs Duck, but I'm going to meet my friend, Fred the Dragon in the village, and we are going to have tea at Mrs Bunn's tea shop," he said.

ELLA MAY MARWOOD aged 10

Joe said goodbye to Mrs Duck and Mr Brown, and went off to meet his friend, Fred the Dragon in the village.

He hadn't gone very far when who should he see, but his friend Annabelle.

"Where are you going?" she asked.

"I'm going to meet Fred," he said.

"May I come too?" asked Annabelle.

"Of course you can," said Joe.

The two friends carried on towards the village.

They hadn't gone much further when they met PC Luca.

"We are going to meet Fred the Dragon in the village. Would you like to come as well?" said Joe.

"Yes please," said PC Luca, and they all walked towards the village together.

Fred the Dragon was delighted to see all three of his very best friends. They all sat down to have a lovely tea, with a delicious chocolate cake that Mrs Bunn had baked especially for them.

When they had finished, Joe said, "I don't know about you, but I am absolutely full up. I think I should go for a walk to let the chocolate cake go down. Would anyone like to come with me?"

We shall all come!" said Fred the Dragon.

The four friends walked along the road until they came to the edge of the village. Just then they heard a trumpet sound. When they turned to see who was playing it, they saw a man on a white horse, with the thickest pair of glasses that you have ever seen.

"Have you seen any soldiers marching around please?" asked the man, holding on to his glasses to stop them falling off his nose.

"We have just come from the village," said PC Luca, and there were no soldiers there."

"Oh dear," said the man, "I don't suppose you would help me look for them, would you?" He asked, polishing his glasses with a huge red handkerchief.

"That's just what I do," said PC Luca. "I look for missing people all the time."

"But this is slightly different," said the man.

"Different?" asked Annabelle.

"Yes, it is a bit," said the man. "You see, I am looking for ten thousand soldiers."

"Ten thousand?" asked Joe. "Goodness me, how can you possibly lose so many people?" he asked. "It does seem a bit careless!"

RUMOR PHOENIX DUFFY aged 10

"It was a bit of a mix up really," said the man. "I said that I would meet them at six o' clock, meaning this morning, and they must have thought I meant six o'clock this evening."

"Well, the little hand of my watch is on the six and the big hand is nearly on the twelve, so it is nearly six o'clock now," said Joe.

"Quiet everybody!" said Fred. "I think I can hear them coming now."

Everyone stopped talking and listened very carefully, and sure enough they could hear the 'tramp, tramp, tramp' of thousands of feet, as the soldiers marched along.

Soon, ten thousand soldiers marched around the corner, and halted in front of the man on his white horse.

"Good evening, men," said the man, peering through his thick glasses. "I'm very sorry for the mix up; I really wanted you all to be here this morning. But now you are here, I would like to march up that hill over there."

"What hill is that?" asked PC Luca. "I do not think there is a hill, there you know."

"I'm sure I saw a hill when I was riding here just now," said the man.

"Why not show us what you saw?" said Joe.

The man rode his horse a little way along the road, and stopped and pointed.

"There it is!" he said.

The four friends burst out laughing; the man was pointing to a haystack! When they told the man what he had seen, he laughed as well.

MICHAEL HOUBART aged 10

Annabelle, Fred the Dragon and PC Luca started to clear away the haystack from the field, while Joe walked back along the road to the village.

Soon they heard a truck coming, and they were all surprised to see Joe with Mr Brown and Mrs Duck. In the truck was the largest pile of earth you have ever seen!

"Mr Brown has brought loads of earth for us to build a hill for you," said Joe.

"And we could not be more delighted," said a very happy Mrs Duck.

"It was a brilliant idea to get rid of all that earth," said Mr Brown.

Everyone lent a hand, and soon the earth had been piled up into quite a high hill.

"There you are," said Joe to the man on the white horse. "There's your hill! Now you can march up and down it as often as you like," he said.

"Thank you very much," said the man. "My name is The Duke of York. Perhaps you have heard of me?" he asked.

"Of course," said the four friends together.

"Why don't you and your soldiers march up and down the hill, while we sing your song?" asked Joe.

So they all sang together, and as they sang, the ten thousand men with the Grand Old Duke of York at their head marched up and down the hill.

When they were so tired they could not march any more they all went to Mrs Bunn's for a huge supper, finishing off with lots of her chocolate cake.

Do you know what the song was that they sang?

The Grand Old Duke of York, he had ten thousand men,

He marched them up to the top of the hill,

 And he marched them down again.

And when they were up they were up,

And when they were down they were down,

And when they were only half way up,

They were neither up nor down.

And they all lived happily ever after.

AMI WOODWARD aged 8

JOE AND THE MAGIC GARDEN

Once upon a time, in a land far, far away, lived a little boy called Joe. Joe lived with his Mummy and Daddy in a house in the country.

One day, Joe was playing in his garden when he heard the sound of flapping wings. Joe smiled to himself, because he knew that his friend Fred the Dragon was on his way. He went running into his house.

"Mummy, Mummy," he shouted, "Fred is here. Can you make a picnic, so that we can have our lunch in the garden please?"

"Of course I can," said Mummy.

By the time Joe went into the garden again, Fred had landed.

"Good to see you Fred," said Joe. "I hope you can stay for lunch. Mummy is making a picnic."

"Ooh yum, yum," said Fred. "All that flying makes me very hungry!"

"Shall we play football"? asked Joe, picking up a ball and setting out the goal posts.

They played football until Mummy and Daddy came out of the house with the picnic.

"Lunch is ready," said Daddy, "and I must get back to doing the gardening."

"We'll put it under the tree for you," said Mummy, and she put lots and lots of food on a picnic rug.

There were boiled eggs and sandwiches, cakes, jelly with ice cream, loads of fruit to finish and lots of fruit juice to drink.

KIA-MARIE WHITTAKER aged 9

"Wow, I'm glad I'm here," said Fred.

The two friends sat under the tree and started to eat. They hadn't been eating very long when they heard someone cough.

"Ahem! Ahem!"

"Did you hear that?" asked Fred.

"I heard someone cough, if that's what you mean," said Joe, "but I can't see who it is."

"Ahem! Ahem," went the cough again, and the two friends looked down to find a little man standing on top of the apple juice bottle.

"Hello," said Joe, "who are you?"

"My name is Doodlebug, and I am King of Gobbleland."

"I've never heard of Gobbleland," said Joe.

"No, not many people have," said the little man called King Doodlebug.

"Is it very far away?" asked Fred.

"Not exactly," said the little man. "In fact, it is right here in your garden."

"What do you mean?" asked Joe.

"You're sitting in it! Gobbleland is a magic kingdom, and only people who have a picnic under this tree on a Sunday afternoon can ever see us."

"How interesting," said Joe.

"We've been waiting a long time for help," said Doodlebug. "You see, we have been having terrible floods in Gobbleland. Every time we build a new house we have to build it on top of a hill, or it gets flooded within a week. In fact it is much worse in the summer."

"Can we help you with your problem?" asked Joe.

MIA FORD aged 8

"I will have to do some magic to make you the right size," said King Doodlebug, pulling a magic wand from his trouser pocket. "Abracadabra," he said.

With a flash and a bang, Joe and Fred the Dragon found themselves standing between the apple juice and the hard boiled eggs, only now they were half the size of a boiled egg.

"Follow me!" said King Doodlebug.

Joe and Fred the Dragon had to run to keep up with Doodlebug as he weaved his way between all the plates of food, which seemed like giant mountains either side of them.

They passed a large green post, which Joe realised was the stem of a flower, and there in front of them was a little village, with shops and a post office and a school.

"There it is: the kingdom of Gobbleland," said King Doodlebug. "It's where I live."

"I can't believe it!" said Fred. "Who would have thought that there was a village built right behind the flower bed, and we've never seen it?"

"I told you. It can only be seen when you have a picnic under the tree on a Sunday afternoon," said King Doodlebug.

Just then it started to rain very hard.

"Oh, oh, here comes the flood again," said King Doodlebug. "We'd better get in the boat."

"What boat?" asked Joe.

"Here it is," said King Doodlebug. Sure enough there was a rowing boat tied to a tree. The three got in just as a big wave came crashing through the flower bed.

"Phew, that was close!" said King Doodlebug. "I've actually been in the village when one of those waves has knocked me over."

They rowed towards the village which had been built on a hill.

King Doodlebug tied the boat to a tree stump, which Joe realised was really a dead weed, and the three walked up the hill to a post office. A man dressed in a red suit came out as they got near. He bowed towards King Doodlebug.

"Good afternoon, Your Majesty."

"Good afternoon, Mr Peasmould. Are you well today?" asked King Doodlebug.

"Wet again," said Mr Peasmould.

"Were you delivering letters near the water again?" asked the King.

"That's right, and I must say I'm getting tired of always getting wet."

King Doodlebug turned to Joe and Fred. "Is there anything you can do for us, to save us from all this water?"

Fred shook his head. "I am not sure that there is anything we can do; after all we can't stop the rain can we?"

Just then a few more drops of rain fell on them.

"Wait a minute," said Joe. "I think I know what is causing your problem. Can you take us back to our picnic and make us our real size again please?" Joe stopped, smiled and gave a little bow, remembering what you have to do in front of a king. "Please, Your Majesty," he said, "I think I can solve your problem."

King Doodlebug's face lit up in a smile. "Do you really have the answer Joe?"

"I most certainly do," said Joe.

" Abracadabra," said King Doodlebug, waving his magic wand.

With a crash and a flash, Joe and Fred the Dragon became their real size again and found themselves sitting with all their lovely picnic things.

Joe turned to Fred the Dragon and said, "wait here a moment, Fred."

Fred was really puzzled but decided that he was also still very hungry and started to eat a boiled egg and a tomato. Joe did not take very long before he came back. He was not alone, with him was Annabelle.

"Over there is where I want it, Annabelle. Will you be able to build it right away please?"

"Of course I can," said Annabelle.

Fred looked on, wondering what on earth Joe had asked Annabelle to build.

Annabelle went to her truck and came back with a large pile of bricks and some cement in her wheelbarrow. Then she got very busy and started to build a wall by the flower bed.

"Let's finish our picnic; I am very hungry," Joe said and started to munch on a carrot.

"Aren't you going to tell me what's going on?" asked Fred the Dragon, with his mouth full of cream cheese and jam sandwich.

"You'll see very soon," said Joe.

They finished some lovely strawberry jelly and vanilla ice cream, and Joe said, "I think I'll have a little sleep under the tree now."

"But what is going on?" Fred asked again. This time there was no reply because Joe was fast asleep.

It seemed to Joe that he had been asleep for only a few minutes when he heard someone calling his name. When he woke up he found it was Annabelle.

"All finished, Joe," she said.

"Thank you, Annabelle," said Joe.

Joe turned to Fred who was getting quite cross, because no one would tell him what was going on. He had also run out of things to eat!

"Come with me," said Joe, and they walked over to where Daddy was doing the gardening. "Just watch my Daddy now."

Daddy picked up the garden hose and started to water the flowers.

"Now do you see why Annabelle has built the wall? Gobbleland is behind the flower bed, and every time Daddy waters the flowers it causes a flood in the village. Annabelle's wall will stop the water from flooding Gobbleland."

"Of course, Joe, you're so clever. Why didn't I think of that?" said Fred.

The next day there was a ring at the door. Bill the postman gave Joe a very, very tiny letter. It was from King Doodlebug and all it said was 'thank you very much'.

And they all lived happily ever after.

JOE AND THE WAFFLES

Once upon a time in a land far, far away lived a little boy called Joe. Joe lived with his Mummy and Daddy in a house in the country.

One day, Joe decided that he would like to visit his friend Fred the Dragon.

Off went Joe to the station and bought a ticket for the ten o'clock train to Dragonland.

DULCIE BELL aged 9

That sounds interesting," said Joe. "I like waffles."

"Why not come with me then?" said Tanky.

"I can't, because I'm going to see my friend, Fred the Dragon and he's expecting me," said Joe.

"Well, why not come afterwards with Fred; I'll give you both a lift on my footplate, and you might get to have a few waffles as well!"

Joe was delighted and, as soon as Tanky arrived at Dragonland station, Joe went in search of his friend.

"Hello, Fred," said Joe, when he found Fred standing outside the station. "Would you like to come and see how waffles are made?"

"That sounds like a brilliant idea," said Fred, who was always hungry.

"Come on then," said Joe. "Tanky is waiting for us."

The two friends climbed aboard the train, and once again Tanky puffed out lots of steam, and soon they were all heading towards the waffle factory.

When they arrived, the owner of the factory was waiting for them. He looked very sad and was crying.

"Whatever is the matter?" asked Joe.

"Oh, Joe, all the waffles have been stolen by a horrible ogre," said the owner.

"Do you know where the ogre went to?" Joe asked.

"All I know is he broke a window and took all the waffles that we had. He then escaped, but I don't know where he went after that."

"How do you know it was an ogre?" asked Fred.

"I saw him as he disappeared around the corner. He was carrying a huge bag, which must have had all the waffles in it."

Just then they heard a steamy noise.

"Whatever is that?" asked the factory owner.

"Why that's, Tanky the train with a load of syrup for the waffles," said Joe.

The owner looked even more upset.

"Oh dear me, whatever am I going to do? All the boys and girls will want their waffles, and all I will have is the syrup with nothing for the syrup to be put on to. What am I going to do, Joe?"

"I'd better put on my thinking cap," said Joe.

Joe thought and thought, and as usual had a brilliant idea.

He turned to his friend, Fred the Dragon and asked if he was ready for a long flight.

"Of course I am. Anything for you, Joe. Where is it you want me to fly to?" he asked.

ELLIE RILY aged 9

"I think most ogres live in Ogreland, so all we have to do is fly there and find the ogre who has a huge supply of waffles. He will be the one who has stolen all of the waffles from the factory."

Fred the Dragon nodded. Joe was always so sensible.

Joe and Fred said goodbye to the factory owner, and as Fred took off with Joe on his back, the owner shouted, "Good luck!"

"Thank you," shouted Fred and Joe, as they took to the sky.

They flew north, over the distant land of Coldington and on towards Icington, until in the distance they could see the lights of Ogreland.

"We'd better land here," said Fred, as they flew over a green clearing. "We don't want the horrible ogres to see us before we manage to find the thief who stole all the waffles do we?"

HARRY NEWBERRY aged 11

"Absolutely not," said Joe.

Fred landed and folded his wings.

"We'd best walk towards the lights, I suppose," said Joe, and off they went.

They passed lots of ogres' houses but not one had a pile of waffles outside.

They began to get very tired and hungry, and when they approached another ogre's house they decided to sit down and rest. Joe and Fred sat on some sacks at the bottom of an ogre's garden and started to think of all the food that they would like to have.

"I would love a big slice of my Mummy's chocolate cake right now," said Fred.

"And I would like a lovely egg sandwich," giggled Joe.

MILLIE KAY aged 9

As Joe spoke, Fred put his hand inside the sack he was sitting on and pulled out a big flat cake looking thing.

"This looks good enough to eat," he said to Joe, and bit into it.

"Why, if I didn't know better I would say it tasted just like a waffle."

"Fred!" shouted Joe. "You've found the waffles. Just look!"

Joe pointed to sack after sack of delicious waffles.

"How are we going to get them back to the owner?" asked Fred.

Again, Joe put on his thinking cap.

"We need to find a telephone," he said. "I forgot to bring mine with me."

Let's go and find one," said Fred, as he unfolded his wings, and Joe climbed on his back once more.

SOPHIE GRAY aged 8

53

They flew towards a village, and sure enough, below them was a telephone box.

Fred landed with a little bump, and Joe called Mr Smith the station master.

"Can you ask Tanky to come right away, please?" he asked.

"That's a bit difficult," said Mr Smith. "You see, he still has all that waffle syrup in his trucks."

"That's absolutely all right," said Joe. "Just send him along to Ogreland station   immediately, please."

Joe climbed onto Fred the Dragon's back and said, "Let's fly back and pick up all the sacks of waffles that we found, and take them to Ogreland station, and wait there for Tanky."

Off they flew and landed in the clearing. Sure enough, all the sacks were there just as they had left them. Joe quickly placed them on to Fred's back."

"Do you think that you can carry all these sacks, as well as me to Ogreland station, Fred?" asked Joe.

"I will certainly try," replied his friend. "I shall have to take a long run-up in order to take off. Hold tight, Joe."

Fred ran and ran until he gathered speed and with a huge grunt of energy he lifted all the sacks of waffles as well as Joe into the air and flew towards the station.

They didn't have to wait very long at the station before Tanky arrived.

"We have to load you up with all the waffles from the wicked ogre, Tanky" said Joe, and Fred started to move the sacks of waffles.

What they did not know was the Ogre had seen Fred fly off and had followed them to the station. When he saw what they were doing he was very angry and shouted for them to stop.

"If you don't give me back all the waffles, I shall have to eat you all up," the Ogre shouted.

Joe went over to one of Tanky's trucks with a jug and poured some syrup into it, and then spread it out onto the path in front of the ogre. When the ogre trod in the syrup he couldn't move and he became stuck in the gooey liquid. Joe, Fred and Tanky were able to take back all the waffles to the owner.

The owner was so pleased that he gave Joe and Fred a lifetime supply of the best waffles you have ever seen.

And they all lived happily ever after.

JOE AND THE WALKING TOWEL

Once upon a time, in a land far, far away, lived a little boy called Joe. Joe lived with his Mummy and Daddy in a house in the country.

One day, Joe was in the bath having a hair wash; he rinsed the shampoo out of his hair and reached for the towel, but it wasn't there. "That's funny, when I got into the bath I put the towel on the chair next to it, and now it has gone," he said.

Joe looked around and saw the towel on the floor. As Joe got out of the bath and reached for it once again, the towel had moved. "This is getting silly: every time I reach for the towel, it's somewhere else!"

"Can't you reach me?" asked the towel.

"Not if you keep moving away," said Joe. "Why won't you let me dry my hair? It's very wet!"

"Oh all right then, I'll do it," said the towel, and it floated up into the air and landed on Joe's head.

"Thank you," said Joe. "But what is the problem? For ages all I've ever done is reach for the towel and dried myself without anything like this happening."

"It's not really a problem," said the towel. "It's just that I was getting bored just sitting around on the towel rail and wanted to do something more exciting."

"Would you like to come out for a walk with me then?" asked Joe.

"Do you mean it?" asked the towel. "Me, go out for a walk with you, Joe? How exciting! I've never ever done anything like that before."

When Joe was dressed he called up to the bathroom, "Are you ready to come for a walk now, Mr Towel?"

To Joe's surprise, the towel came running down the stairs. "I'm ready! Let's go!" he said excitedly.

Joe and the towel set off for the village. They had not gone very far before they came to the duck pond. Mrs Duck was getting out of the water.

"Hello, Mrs Duck," said Joe. "How are you today?"

"I'm wet," said Mrs Duck.

"Let me dry you off then," said a voice.

"Who said that?" asked Mrs Duck.

"That was my new friend, the walking towel," said Joe.

"Walking towel?" asked Mrs Duck. "That's silly."

"I'll show you silly," said the towel, and landed on Mrs Duck's wet feathers, and quickly dried them.

"Thank you very much," said a surprised Mrs Duck.

"Don't mention it," said the towel, as he carried on walking towards the village with Joe. They hadn't gone very far when they heard Mrs Cow mooing in her barn.

"Hello, Mrs Cow," said Joe. "How are you today?"

"I'm all wet," she said. "The farmer spilt milk over me, and now I'm soaking."

"I'll dry you," said a voice.

"Who said that?" asked Mrs Cow.

"It was the walking towel," said Joe.

"Walking towel? Don't be ridiculous!" said Mrs Cow.

"I'll show you ridiculous," said the walking towel, and landed on Mrs Cow's back and started to dry her.

"How amazing! I've never been dried by a walking towel before," said Mrs Cow, "Thank you."

"You're welcome," said the walking towel, and carried on walking towards the village with Joe.

"You don't seem to be walking very fast now," said Joe.

"That's because I'm all wet," said the towel. "The water from Mrs Duck and the milk from Mrs Cow have settled in my towel and made me soaking wet. As I am wet, I'm heavier and because I'm heavier, I'm slower," he said.

"We need to dry you out," said Joe, and he put his thinking cap on. "I know, I'll call my friend, Fred the Dragon and see if he can come over right away," said Joe. Joe called his friend, Fred the Dragon. Fred was delighted to fly over immediately.

Meanwhile, Joe and the walking towel arrived at Mrs Bunn's tea shop.

"Would you like to have some tea and cake?" asked Joe.

"Yes please," said Mr Towel and then he stopped and looked very puzzled.

"What is tea and cake?" he asked.

"Haven't you ever had tea and cake?" asked Joe.

"All I've ever done," said the walking towel, "is to sit on your towel rail, waiting to be used," he said.

"Then you shall have the largest cup of tea and the biggest slice of cake to make up for it," said Joe. Joe and Mr Towel sat down at a table outside Mrs Bunn's tea shop.

"What would you like today?" asked Mrs Bunn.

"May we please have two large cups of tea and a huge slice of chocolate cake for my friend the walking towel," Joe asked.

"Walking towel? I've never heard of a walking towel before! I must say, I could use a towel right now to mop up all the puddles in my tea shop," said Mrs Bunn.

"I'll do it," said Mr Towel, and immediately walked over to the tea room and wiped up all the puddles. Mrs Bunn was so pleased that she gave Joe and the walking towel two enormous slices of cake and a cup of tea each.

"That was delicious," said the walking towel, when he had finished the cake. "The trouble is, what with mopping up all the puddles in the tea shop, drying Mrs Cow's back and Mrs Duck's feathers, I've got so much liquid inside me I can't move at all now."

Just then they heard a flapping noise and they looked up to see Fred the Dragon flying towards them.

"Hello, Joe," said Fred, "What can I do for you?"

"I need you to breathe hot air on my friend the walking towel," said Joe.

"Walking towel? Don't be silly. There's no such thing," said Fred

"Oh yes there is," said a voice.

"Who said that?" asked Fred.

"It was me," said the Towel. "Only I can't move because I have become so wet. I dried out all of Mrs Bunn's puddles and dried Mrs Cow's back as well as Mrs Duck's feathers. I have just eaten a huge slice of chocolate cake and drunk a big cup of tea."

"You poor thing," said Fred. "Now, just stand over there and I'll see what I can do."

Fred huffed and puffed and soon was breathing out very hot air from his mouth; he turned his head towards the walking towel and quickly dried him.

"I'm dry," said Mr Towel. "Thank you very much, Fred," he said and then he turned to Joe.

"Joe?" he asked.

"What is it, Mr Towel?" asked Joe.

"Do you think I can go back to the bathroom and sit on your towel rail; it really is too exciting to be out in the village, and I would rather have a sleep on your towel rail."

Joe laughed and then said, "Of course you can."

Joe and the walking towel climbed onto Fred's back and were soon flying over Joe's house.

When they got inside, Joe's Mummy said to Joe, "Why did you take the towel away, Joe?"

"That's a long story," he said, and smiled at his friend, Fred the Dragon as they put the walking towel back on the towel rail. "Night, night, Mr Towel," said Joe, but there was no reply; the walking towel was fast asleep, waiting for Joe to have his next bath.

Fred and Joe went to play in the garden, and Mummy looked at the walking towel. "That's funny," she said, "the towel is covered in chocolate. I'd better wash it." And so saying, she took the walking towel off the towel rail and put him in the washing machine.

"That's more like it," thought Mr Towel. "I don't ever want to go for a walk again, it's far too tiring!"

And they all lived happily ever after.

EMILEE CLEAVER aged 10

JOE AND LAVENDER FARM

Once upon a time, in a land far, far away, lived a little boy called Joe. Joe lived with his Mummy and Daddy in a house in the country.

One day, when the sun was nice and warm, Fred the Dragon called Joe to see if he would like to go to Lavender Farm for the day.

"That's a good idea," said Joe. "I've been wondering what to do on such a lovely day as this."

"I'll fly over right away and we can get to Lavender Farm in time for the tractor ride," said Fred.

Joe raced into the bathroom, had a wash, cleaned his teeth and then rushed into his bedroom and put on his going to the farm clothes.

"What time is Fred picking you up?" asked Mummy.

"He said he would fly over right away," said Joe, and just then there was a ring at the door.

"I think he's here now," said Daddy.

Joe ran downstairs and opened the door. Sure enough, there was Fred, as large as life.

"I hope I didn't keep you waiting too long, Joe," said Fred.

LIAM STERLING aged 10

63

Joe laughed because it was always good to see his friend, and he enjoyed knowing that Fred could fly, because he was a dragon.

"Will you give me a ride on your back to Lavender Farm?" asked Joe.

"I certainly will," said Fred. "Are you ready to go now?"

Joe turned to his Mummy and Daddy. "What time would you like me to come home?" He asked.

"Be home in time for supper," said Mummy.

"I will," said Joe, and he kissed his Mummy and Daddy goodbye and climbed onto his friend Fred the Dragon's back.

Fred took a long run up the garden path and was soon high up over the roofs of the houses and on his way to Lavender Farm with Joe on his back. They hadn't flown very far before they could hear someone whistling.

"Can you hear anything?" said Fred.

"Do you mean that whistling?" asked Joe.

"It's very strange but I think it's coming from above us," said Fred.

Joe looked up, and there just above him was little Robin Redbreast.

"Hello, Robin," said Joe, "Why are you whistling so loudly?"

"I've been trying to get your attention," said Robin. "We've got trouble down below and we need your help, Joe."

"Take us down fast," said Joe to Fred, and Fred dived down with Robin just behind. They landed with a bit of a bump.

"Sorry about that," said Fred. "I was trying out my new quick landing idea but it still needs working on."

"As long as we land safely, it doesn't matter," said Joe. "Now what's the trouble, Robin?" asked Joe.

"Come with me and I'll show you," said Robin, and he hopped along the edge of a field and went through a gate. There in front of him was a tiny house, and on the doorstep of the house were ten empty green bottles.

"That's the problem," said Robin.

"I don't understand," said Fred. "All I can see are empty bottles."

"And that's the problem," said Robin. "You see, I live in the house with my family, and we all like a glass of milk before we go to bed. Once a day without fail, Sid the milkman comes along in his truck and leaves enough milk for me and my family, but we haven't seen Sid for days and the bottles are too heavy for me to pick up, and we've run out of milk."

"Don't you worry," said Joe, "I think I know a way to help you. Now, Fred, do you think that you can fly me to the police station? I need to see PC Luca."

"Of course I can," said Fred.

"You wait here Robin and we'll be back very soon," said Joe, as he climbed on to Fred's back and took off into the sky.

"Do you know which way to go?" asked Fred.

"You see the traffic lights down there," said Joe pointing towards the town on their left.

"I certainly can," said Fred.

"Turn left and follow the road, and it will bring us right up to the police station," said Joe.

"That's what I like about you Joe: you're so clever," said Fred, as he turned left and followed the road.

Soon, they could see the police station, and Joe said to Fred, "There it is Fred! Let's land now, but not one of your special, quick landings this time!"

"Don't you worry," said Fred, laughing, "I'll have us down nice and safely."

SAM CHALLIS aged 9

PC Luca was in his back garden, behind the police station; imagine his surprise when a huge dragon with Joe on his back came sweeping down out of the sky and nearly landed on top of him.

"Goodness gracious me!" said PC Luca. "You nearly scared me out of my uniform. Why, it's Joe and Fred the Dragon. What can I do for you today?"

"Our friend, Robin Redbreast has not had any milk delivered by Sid the milkman for a long time," said Joe, "and because the bottles are so big, Robin can't go to the supermarket to get any more, and he needs Sid to take him his milk every day, and..." Joe stopped talking, because he could see that PC Luca was getting very upset.

"Is there anything the matter, PC Luca?" asked Joe.

"I'm afraid there is; you see Joe, it's all my fault. Sid the milkman went on holiday and asked me to take the milk to Robin and his family, and I just didn't know where to get milk from, and then I'm afraid I forgot about it. I'm so sorry."

"Well, why don't we put everything right and get the milk now, and take it to Robin right away," said Joe.

"But you don't understand," said PC Luca. "I don't have any milk and I don't know where to get it."

Joe laughed and laughed." Come on PC Luca. Come with me and Fred, and we will show you where to get the milk."

So PC Luca climbed onto Fred's back, and Joe got on behind him.

"You know where we're going to get the milk don't you?" Joe asked Fred.

"Of course I do," answered Fred.

"Lavender Farm," Joe and Fred said at the same time.

Off Fred flew and soon they landed at the farm.

Joe asked Mrs Cow if he could have a few bottles of milk for Robin, and of course, she was only too delighted to help out.

"Why don't you come and have a ride on me while you are waiting," said Louise the Tractor.

And off they all went for a lovely ride around the farm. By the time they had finished the ride, Mrs Cow was waiting with a basket full of bottles of milk.

They all waved goodbye to Mrs Cow and Louise and were soon in the sky, on their way to Robin Redbreast's house. On the way they stopped at the police station, so that PC Luca could get off. "Be sure to say sorry from me to Robin and his family, won't you, Joe," said PC Luca.

"Don't you worry, I will," said Joe.

Robin Redbreast was delighted with the milk and said he would call PC Luca and tell him not to worry about saying sorry. "Anyone could have forgotten," Robin said, "and no harm was done. Now, how about you both stay for supper?" Robin asked.

I don't know about PC Luca and his memory, but I've just remembered that Mummy asked me to be home in time for supper at my house," said Joe, "so we'd better go, but thank you all the same."

"No, thank *you* Joe. I don't know what we would have done without you being so clever," said Robin.

Joe climbed up once again onto Fred's back. "Goodbye Robin," said the two friends together as they zoomed up into the sky and flew home for supper.

And they all lived happily ever after.

ANDREW HUNT aged 9

JOE AND TANKY THE TRAIN

Once upon a time, in a land far, far away, lived a little boy called Joe. Joe lived with his Mummy and Daddy in a house in the country.

One day, Joe's Daddy asked him if he would like to go to the station, to see the trains.

"Will Tanky be there?" Joe asked.

"Would you like him to be?" asked Daddy.

"Yes I would, please," said Joe.

"Then why don't you call Mr Smith, the Station Master and see if he can come?"

Joe immediately called Mr Smith and was very pleased that Tanky was just as eager to see Joe as Joe was to see Tanky.

"I'll let you know what time to be at the station," said Mr Smith.

Joe's Mummy called up the stairs to ask if Joe and Daddy would like to take a packed lunch with them.

"No thank you," said Joe's Daddy. "We'll have lunch at the station."

Just then the phone rang. "You'd better answer it Joe," said Daddy.

When Joe answered the phone, he was delighted to hear that Mr Smith had arranged for Tanky to meet him and his Daddy at the station, at ten o'clock.

"What time is it now?" asked Joe.

"The little hand is on the nine and the big hand is on the twelve," said Daddy.

JOSHUA BAKER aged 11

As quick as a flash, Joe answered, "It's nine o'clock!"

"Quite right," said Daddy. "That's exactly the right time, so we had better hurry if we are to be at the station in, how long, Joe?"

"One hour of course," said Joe.

"Exactly," said Daddy.

Joe went into the bathroom and cleaned his teeth, then into his bedroom where he put on his special going to the station clothes. He went downstairs, where Mummy gave him a lovely breakfast, and soon it was time to leave with his Daddy for the station.

"Shall we take a camera?" asked Daddy.

"Good idea," said Joe, and off they went, waving goodbye to Mummy as they left the house.

When they got to the station, Mr Clip, the ticket collector looked very happy to see Joe.

"I'm glad you could come," he said. "Do you know who's coming into the station soon?"

"Of course I do," said Joe. "If I'm not mistaken, it will be Tanky the Train at ten o'clock."

"I'm amazed that you know that," said Mr Clip.

Daddy laughed, "It's because of Joe that he is coming."

"Really?" said Mr Clip.

JEREMY BEARD aged 10

Without another word, Joe called George the Signalman.

"I can see him coming now," said George. "What would you like me to do, Joe?"

"Can you divert him to a side junction so that the buffers at the end can stop him?" said Joe.

"I'll certainly try," said George the Signalman and immediately pulled a

72

lever that moved the rails in front of Tanky, who by this time was going faster than ever.

Sure enough, the rail in front of Tanky moved, just in time to divert Tanky onto the side junction and, seconds later, Tanky hit the buffers with an enormous bang and a cloud of steam. George the signalman called Joe on his phone immediately.

"I can't see anything just yet because the steam is so thick... Wait a minute, the steam is clearing; oh good, your idea worked Joe; Tanky is stopped and I want you to come right away to see what the matter is."

"I'm coming now. Goodbye George, I'll see you soon, and thank you very much," said Joe.

Then Joe called his friend, PC Luca. "There's an emergency, PC Luca: Tanky nearly had an accident and I need to get to the junction with my Daddy, very quickly."

"I'm on my way," said PC Luca, and in a flash was at the station, picking up Joe and his Daddy. They said goodbye to Mr Smith, the Station Master, who had joined Mr Clip on the platform and zoomed off, with PC Luca's siren making an enormous noise. Soon, they arrived at the junction and there was Tanky being cleaned down by George the Signalman.

"If it hadn't been for you, Joe, I don't know what would have happened," said

Tanky. "My brakes jammed and I couldn't stop. If you hadn't called George the Signalman I would have crashed."

"He is one of the cleverest people I know," said PC Luca.

"But how are we going to get the brakes mended?" asked George the Signalman.

"Do you know anyone who can repair them?" asked Joe's Daddy.

"Yes, I do," said Joe, and very quickly called his friend, Dan the Mechanic.

"Now don't you worry," said Dan. "I'll have Tanky right as rain just as quickly as I can. Why don't you and Daddy go and have your lunch and by the time you finish I'll have fixed the brakes."

"Thanks, Dan," said Joe, and he went off with his Daddy and had a lovely lunch. As soon as they had finished they went back to the junction and there was Tanky, all sparkling and clean, with his brakes mended and ready to go.

"Let's have a photograph with all of us in it, shall we?" said Daddy.

"I'll take it," said George the Signalman.

Then Tanky suggested that he gave them all a ride back to the station.

Imagine the surprise on Mr Smith the Station Master's face, when Dan, Daddy, George the Signalman and, of course, Joe all arrived together at the station.

Everyone agreed that they had had quite an adventure, and Joe and his Daddy were delighted when Mummy arrived at the station in her car to collect them and take them home for tea.

And they all lived happily ever after.

JOE AND THE WASHING LINE

Once upon a time, in a land far, far away, lived a little boy called Joe. Joe lived with his Mummy and Daddy in a house in the country.

One day, Joe was helping his Mummy with the washing. Mummy had put all the washing in the washing machine and Joe was hanging it up in the garden to dry. The washing line stretched from the back of Joe's house to the bottom of the garden.

Joe started by hanging the clothes on the line nearest to the house and as the line filled up he moved further and further towards the bottom of the garden, but he realized that he didn't have enough clothes pegs to hang out all the washing.

Joe asked his Mummy for more pegs, but she did not have any, so Joe put on his thinking cap and came up with an answer.

"I'll use paper clips," he thought.

He went into Daddy's study and asked Daddy for some paper clips.

"You'd better have big ones," Daddy said, "otherwise the washing will blow away in the wind."

Joe took the paper clips and finished off the job of hanging the washing out to dry. Then, Mummy called to say that she still had a few things to hang out. Joe was just going back into the house when the telephone rang: it was his friend Fred the Dragon.

"Would you like to come and play with me?" Fred asked.

Joe asked his Mummy, who said that he could go as soon as all the washing was hung out to dry.

Joe told Fred what he had to do for his Mummy.

CHISEMBELE BWAYLA aged 11

"As soon as I've finished, I'll take the very next train. I should be with you at about one o'clock," he said.

"I'll have lunch waiting for you," said Fred.

Off went Joe and finished hanging out the clothes with the paper clips.

As he finished, he said out loud, "Now I can get the train to Dragonland."

"No you can't," said a voice.

"I'm sorry, did someone say something?" said Joe in the general direction of the voice.

"Yes, I said, 'no you can't'."

"Who is that?"

"It's me, the Washing Line," said the voice.

"The Washing Line?" said Joe. "That's very strange; I've never heard of a washing line talking before."

"I've never heard of anyone putting up washing with paper clips before either," said the Washing Line.

"So why can't I go to Dragonland?" said Joe.

"Because I need to have real pegs for the washing," said the Washing Line.

"That's all very well," said Joe, "but there aren't any anywhere. After all, why do you think I used paper clips in the first place? I looked everywhere but there were no pegs to be found and that's why I used

DREW FISHER aged 11

"Which way did he go?" asked Joe.

The Woodcutter's wife pointed Joe in the right direction and Joe was soon walking along a path in the forest, looking for the wood cutter.

He hadn't gone very far, when he came across a clearing.

77

There was the Woodcutter, looking through the window of a house.

"Hello," said Joe. "Are you the Woodcutter?"

"That's me," said the Woodcutter, "but you'll have to excuse me and talk to me later; you see I am looking for my children, Hansel and Gretel, and I think they are inside this house as prisoners of a Wicked Witch."

"I know all about Wicked Witches," said Joe. "If you need me to help you, just let me know."

"I would like you to help me please," said the Woodcutter. "Can you help me rescue my Hansel and Gretel?"

"My pleasure," said Joe.

Joe knocked on the door and the Wicked Witch answered it.

"Are there two children inside, called Hansel and Gretel?" Joe asked.

"Certainly. I have them, and I'm going to eat them for my supper!" said the Wicked Witch.

"For your supper?" asked Joe. "Yuck! I can't think of anything worse. Why not have some cheese on toast or scrambled egg? I'm sure that would taste nicer," he said.

"Do you think so?" said the Wicked Witch.

"I'm sure of it," said Joe. "If you let me in, I'll cook you some lovely scrambled eggs on toast, just the way my Mummy and Daddy cook them," he said.

"Come in then," said the Wicked Witch, hungrily.

As Joe entered, he looked around and saw the two children hanging in a cage from the ceiling.

"Don't worry," he whispered to them. "I'll soon have you out of there; be patient."

Joe walked over to the stove and soon was making some lovely, scrumptious, scrambled eggs. Joe noticed that the witch had lots of magical potions in her kitchen, and when the Wicked Witch wasn't looking, he sprinkled some Being Nice Powder all over the eggs.

"Here you are," he said, and put the eggs and toast in front of the Wicked Witch.

As she ate the eggs, her dark face became bright and lovely. Soon her hair became a golden colour.

"I must say, these are the nicest eggs I have ever eaten," she said.

When she had finished and had lots of Being Nice Powder, she said, "I can't think why those children are hanging up in a cage in my kitchen. Will you let them go please, Joe?"

Joe smiled. "Of course I will," he said.

GRACE BORONTE aged 10

He cut the rope and lowered the cage to the ground and opened the cage door for Hansel and Gretel.

The Wicked Witch, who was of course no longer wicked, watched with a smile on her face as Joe waved to her. The Witch said goodbye to Joe and Hansel and Gretel.

Joe took the children back to their father who was delighted to see them.

As they were walking back through the forest, the Woodcutter asked Joe how he could possibly repay his wonderful good deed.

"Well since you are a Woodcutter, I need loads and loads of clothes pegs; can you make me some please?"

"It will be my pleasure," said the Woodcutter.

When they got to the clearing in the forest, the Woodcutter's wife was so pleased with Joe for bringing back Hansel and Gretel, she asked Joe whether she could cook something for him to thank him for helping rescue Hansel and Gretel.

"I'd rather not have scrambled eggs, if you don't mind," said Joe, smiling.

Finally Joe arrived home and went out to the washing line with all the new clothes pegs.

"Can you change all the washing that has paper clips with the new clothes pegs please, Joe?" asked the Washing Line.

"Of course I can," said Joe, and did exactly that. Joe took off all the paper clips which he gave back to his Daddy and hung all the washing out with the new clothes pegs instead.

"And now, if you don't mind, I would like to catch the train for Dragonland," said Joe.

"Thank you, Joe; of course, you should get the train," said the Washing Line.

Off Joe went to the station, and when Mr Smith the station master saw him, he asked if Tanky could take Joe himself.

"My pleasure," said Tanky.

When Joe arrived at Dragonland, Fred looked a little sad.

"Whatever is the matter?" Joe asked.

"I was coming back from the village with our tea, when I dropped the bag with all the shopping in a puddle and everything is ruined," said Fred.

"Oh, that's all right," said Joe, holding up a huge bag.

"What's in the bag?" asked Fred.

"Why, it's the biggest Chocolate cake you have ever seen," laughed Joe. "The Woodcutter's wife made it for me for rescuing Hansel and Gretel."

JAMES FERRARI aged 11

"Whatever are you talking about?" said Fred the Dragon.

"It's a long story," said Joe. "Just eat up, Fred," said Joe, biting into the delicious cake, "and I'll tell you all about it."

So Fred and all his family gathered round for tea with Joe, and they ate the Woodcutter's wife's delicious chocolate cake until it was time for bed.

And they all lived happily ever after.

JOE AND HUMPTY DUMPTY

Once upon a time in a land far, far away lived a little boy called Joe. Joe lived with his Mummy and Daddy in a house in the country.

One day, Joe was walking down a country lane, singing a nursery rhyme.

"Humpty Dumpty sat on a wall, Humpty Dumpty had a great fall..."

"No I didn't," said a voice.

Joe looked up to see a rather round and certainly very cheerful person sitting on a wall at the side of the road.

POPPY McCARTHY aged 9

"You didn't?" asked Joe. "But all the songs I have ever heard always say that you had a great fall."

"Well, that's what they sing," said Humpty Dumpty, "but people always get that bit wrong; I suppose it's because they don't know what I know."

"What do you know that others, do not?" asked Joe.

"What do you think I am?" asked Humpty.

"I beg your pardon?" asked Joe. "What do you mean?"

"A simple question," said Humpty. "What am I?"

"It seems to me that you are a rather large egg," said Joe.

"Exactly," said Humpty, "and that is my point."

"I don't follow you," said Joe.

"Being an egg is bad enough; I mean anyone could push you, and your shell would break if you didn't take care, and that's why I say, I know what others do not."

Joe, by this time, was getting more and more puzzled. Humpty looked at Joe and saw the look on his face.

"Oh, I'm sorry, Joe, let me explain. You see, in the nursery rhyme, everyone sings 'Humpty Dumpty sat on a wall, Humpty Dumpty had a great fall; all the king's horses and all the king's men couldn't put Humpty together again'. Now, as you see, here I am: not broken, not in bits, but in one whole and very oval piece."

"Yes, now that is a puzzle," said Joe.

"The reason is quite simple really," said Humpty. "I was hard boiled when I was growing up, so my shell won't break, and when the king's men tried to push me off the wall, I just ran away, and ever since they have been chasing me to try and push me off the wall, to see if they can get me to break, and I've been hiding from them ever since."

"Are they still after you?" asked Joe.

"I haven't heard them for quite some time, but I'm sure sooner or later I'll...." Humpty stopped and then listened. "I think I hear them now. Excuse me, Joe, while I hide on the other side of this wall." So saying, Humpty rolled off the wall and dropped down behind it so that he could not be seen.

Sure enough, Joe heard an enormous clip clop of hooves and who should come around the corner, but a hundred horsemen, all dressed in the King's uniform.

When the leader saw Joe he asked, "Have you seen a broken egg please Joe?"

Because Joe always tells the truth, he was able to answer honestly, "No I haven't," because, of course, Humpty was not broken.

"Thank you," said the leader. "Come on men, off we go!" he shouted, and all the King's men disappeared around the corner.

"Phew, that was close!" said Humpty, looking over the wall at Joe. "Now what am I going to do to make sure they can't catch me?" he asked.

Joe put on his thinking cap and smiled as he always does when he has a brilliant idea.

"I am going to take you somewhere where the king's men will never think of looking," said Joe. "Let me help you down from the wall, and we can go to the train station."

Joe helped Humpty down from the wall, and the two of them walked along the country lane towards the station.

They hadn't gone very far, when they heard the sound of a car coming.

"Do you think you should hide?" asked Joe.

"Oh no, that won't be the King's men: they only ever chase me on horses," said Humpty.

AG NE JOCERYTE aged 8

Just then a car came into sight, and what a good sight it was!

"It's my friend, PC Luca, in his new police car," said Joe.

"Good morning, Joe," said PC Luca, "and who have we here? I must say you look like someone I should know."

"This is Humpty Dumpty," said Joe.

PC Luca raised his hat and said, "Of course! How do you do?"

"I'm quite well, thanks to your friend, Joe," said Humpty.

"Have you had trouble, Joe?" asked PC Luca.

Joe told PC Luca all about the King's men and how they were chasing Humpty to try to push him off the wall.

"Why that is not right," said PC Luca. "We don't allow people to push others. I will have to help you; the trouble is that I don't think you will fit into my police car," said PC Luca, looking at the rather large egg shape of Humpty Dumpty.

"We need to get to the station," said Joe. "I want to take Humpty to a special place where the king's men will not think of looking for him," he said.

"In that case, I shall drive very slowly in front of you, all the way to the station, so that I can make sure no harm comes to you," said PC Luca.

"Thank you, PC Luca," said Humpty. "That makes me feel very safe indeed. I have your police car in front of me and Joe walking with me. Thank you very much."

Off the friends went to the station. They hadn't gone very far before Joe saw his friend, Annabelle, walking towards them, carrying her tool bag.

"Hello, Joe," said Annabelle. "Where are you going?"

"I am taking Humpty Dumpty to the station, with PC Luca," he said.

ALA KALINSKA aged 8

"Why are you and PC Luca looking after Humpty Dumpty, Joe?" She asked.

So Joe told her all about Humpty and the King's men, and how they were going to the station so that Joe could take Humpty to a place where the king's men would not think of looking for Humpty.

"I'll come along with you then, just to make sure that you have lots of people to help you guard Humpty," said Annabelle.

So the four friends carried along the country lane until they came to the duck pond.   On the pond were Mr and Mrs Duck and all their ducklings.

"Hello, Joe," said Mrs Duck.   "Where are you and your friends going on such a nice morning?"

When Joe told her, she insisted that she and Mr Duck and their whole family came along as well.

By the time they reached the village, Joe had gathered around him so many people that there were hundreds of friends, all marching along to help protect Humpty Dumpty. But before they could reach the station, Humpty said to Joe, "I can hear horses again."

Sure enough, all the king's men were waiting for them.

ELLA HALE aged 9

"Why have you got so many people with you, Humpty?" asked the leader.

"We are here to protect Humpty Dumpty," said Joe. "If you try to push him we will be very cross," he said.

The leader looked very frightened and turned to all his men and said, "I

think we should leave Humpty Dumpty alone forever and ever because I didn't know he had so many friends." With that, all the King's men rode away, never to be seen again.

"How can I ever thank all of you for protecting me, and especially you, Joe, for asking everyone to come along with us to the station?" Humpty said.

"You are very welcome," said Joe. "But just to be on the safe side, I still would like to take you to a place where the King's men will never find you."

JESSICA MARWOOD aged 8

Joe and Humpty said goodbye to all their friends and he and PC Luca and Annabelle walked into the station, where Mr Smith was waiting for them.

When Joe told Mr Smith the story of how they had frightened away all the king's men, Mr Smith said that they must have free tickets to travel anywhere that Joe wanted to go. Joe whispered to Mr Smith where it was, and Mr Smith nodded.

"I agree Joe; that is a very good place indeed, and the King's men would never think of going there," he said.

So Joe went to the ticket window and was given four tickets: one for PC Luca, one for Annabelle, one for Humpty Dumpty and of course one for himself.

The four friends waited patiently on the platform with Mr Smith, for the next train to arrive.

Soon they heard Tanky chuffing along. heading for the station.

"Here comes the train now," said Mr Smith.

"But where are you taking me?" asked Humpty Dumpty.

"To Dragonland," said Joe, "where my friend, Fred the Dragon will see that no harm ever comes to you."

Off went the train with the four friends on board, and Mr Smith waved goodbye to them.

And they all lived happily ever after.

ELISE VOYCE aged 9

JOE AND THE WATERY MAZE

Once upon a time, in a land far, far away, lived a little boy called Joe. Joe lived with his Mummy and Daddy in a house in the country.

One day, Joe decided to visit his friend Fred the Dragon. He went to the station and there was Mr Smith the station master.

"Hello, Joe," he said, "I haven't seen you for ages. Where are you going today?"

"I'm going to Dragonland to see my friend, Fred the Dragon," said Joe.

"We shall have to have Tanky take you, because you are a very good boy and good boys always have special treats." So saying, Mr Smith called Tanky on the telephone.

"Anything for Joe, I'm coming right away," said Tanky.

Soon, Joe was very pleased to see his friend racing around the corner.

"Where would you like to go today?" asked Tanky.

"To Dragonland please, Tanky," said Joe.

"Climb on board and we'll be off," said Tanky.

Joe climbed onto Tanky's foot plate and soon they were speeding along the countryside. They hadn't gone very far, when they saw someone standing at the side of the railway, waving a big red flag.

"I'd better stop," said Tanky.

When they stopped, they saw that it was PC Luca.

"I'm glad you stopped," said PC Luca.

"How can we help you?" asked Tanky.

PC Luca turned to Joe and said, "I heard you were going to Dragonland."

"That's right," said Joe.

"Can you take me along as well, because I've got to get to Dragonland; I have to meet with PC Dragon to talk about the traffic that they are expecting, because of the summer party."

"No problem, climb on board," said Tanky.

Soon, the friends were racing off into the countryside.

Fred the Dragon was waiting at Dragonland station.

Tanky raced into the station and showed off just a little bit, by screeching to a halt. He only just managed to stop in time. "Whoops!" he said, as his engine nearly hit the buffers.

"Thank you for the ride Tanky," said Joe, as he stepped onto the platform. Joe waved goodbye to Tanky, and Tanky reversed out of the station and disappeared around the corner.

"Good to see you, Joe," said Fred. "Hello, PC Luca. Are you here to play with Joe and me?" asked Fred.

"No, I'm here to meet with PC Dragon," said PC Luca. "I have to arrange for all the boys and girls to go to the Watery Maze summer party."

"We'll see you later then," said Joe.

PC Luca waved goodbye, and was soon on his way to the Dragonland police station. Fred turned to Joe and asked him what he would like to do today.

"Shall we go to the Watery Maze?" Joe asked.

"What a good idea," said Fred.

ISAAC WHITE aged 9

Off the two friends went. When they got to the Watery Maze, Mr Jones, the man in charge, said that there was a problem.

"You see," he said, "I haven't got any boats for you to travel in, because there is a horrible scarecrow that lives in the maze and he keeps stealing all the boats and hiding them in the middle of the maze, and I've only got my own boat left."

"If you let us have your boat, we will try to help you get all the others back," said Joe.

Mr Jones said that he would be very happy if Joe and Fred could help him, because the summer party was happening that afternoon, and they would need all the boats for all the boys and girls. Joe and Fred got into Mr Jones's boat and were soon rowing along the first part of the Watery Maze.

"Be sure to count the dead ends," shouted Mr Jones. "There are ten before you get to the middle of the maze."

"We will!" shouted Joe.

As they entered the Watery Maze, Fred saw a long watery path in front of them.

"Let's row along there!" he said.

They hadn't gone very far, before they saw the horrible scarecrow waiting for them.

"We'd better turn around," said Fred.

"That was dead end number one," said Joe.

As they quickly turned the boat around, the scarecrow shouted after them.

"You can't get away from me that easily. I want your boat."

Joe pulled on the oars and they were soon out of sight of the horrible scarecrow.

"Phew, that was close!" Shall we try that way?" said Fred, pointing to another watery pathway.

Off they went and hadn't gone very far before they met Mrs Quack and her family of ducklings.

"Hello, who are you?" Mrs Quack asked.

"I am Fred the Dragon, and this is my best friend, Joe," he said.

"I'm very pleased to meet you, I'm Mrs Quack and I think you should

know that there is a horrible scarecrow who is taking all the boats," she said.

"Yes, we know," said Joe "this boat belongs to Mr Jones, and we have come to get all of his boats back."

"I see," said Mrs Quack. "Did you know that all the boats have been hidden at the centre of the Watery Maze?"

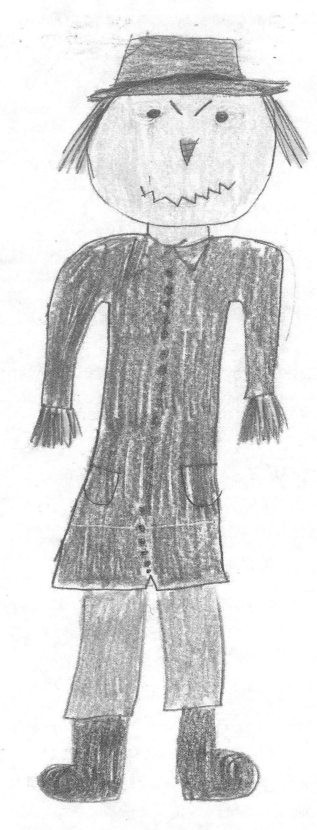

MIA SPRINGER aged 9

"Yes, we were told that," said Joe, "and we were also told that there were ten dead ends before we could get to the middle."

"That's right," said Mrs Quack. "That also means that there are ten chances for the horrible scarecrow to steal your boat before you get there."

"Can you help us?" asked Joe, "As you live here, you must know all the right directions."

"Follow me," said Mrs Quack. "I'll show you the way, but you must be very quiet, if the horrible scarecrow hears you, he will come out of the dead end and steal your boat."

So, Joe and Fred followed Mrs Quack and her family.

"Would you please count all the dead ends we go past?" Mrs Quack asked.

Off they all went, and soon they passed another pathway.

"Number two," shouted Fred.

"Shush!" said Joe. "Not so loud, or the horrible scarecrow will hear us."

"Sorry," said Fred, and whispered, "That was number two."

Joe nodded, and they carried on rowing along the Water Maze behind Mrs Quack and her family. Fred had counted eight pathways, when there was a loud crash and the horrible scarecrow came wading through the water towards them.

"Can you row any faster?" Fred asked Joe. "I think he is going to catch us," he shouted.

Joe pulled on the oars as hard as he could, and soon they left the horrible scarecrow far behind them.

"What number are we up to?" asked Mrs Quack.

"Um, oh dear, I've forgotten," said Fred.

"I think the last number you said was eight," said Joe.

"I hope you are right, Joe," said Mrs Quack, "because if you are, there is only one last dead end to get past before we have reached the middle."

They were nearly there, when Fred shouted, "There's number nine!"

"You mustn't shout so loudly," said Mrs Quack. "The horrible scarecrow will hear you."

"Too late," said Joe. "There he is."

Standing in their way was the horrible scarecrow.

"Oh dear," said Fred. "I'm sorry I was so noisy. What are we going to do, Joe? The horrible scarecrow will steal this last boat, and we will never be able to get all the boats back for the boys and girls. Put on your thinking cap quickly."

Joe thought and thought and then had a great idea. Just as the horrible scarecrow was walking towards them, he turned to Mrs Quack.

"Mrs Quack, can you and your family swim to the horrible scarecrow and peck at his straw body?"

"Of course we can. Come on," she said to her ducklings.

All the ducks swam to the horrible scarecrow and began to peck away at the straw. Slowly but surely the scarecrow got smaller and smaller as the ducks pulled out the straw from his body. Soon, the only thing left was the horrible scarecrow's hat, floating down the Watery Maze.

"Well done," shouted Joe.

"It was all down to you, Joe and your quick thinking," said Mrs Quack.

"There's dead end number ten," whispered Fred.

"You don't have to whisper anymore!" shouted Joe, and they all laughed, because there in front of them were all the boats.

MIA SPRINGER aged 9

"How are we going to get so many boats back to Mr Jones?" Asked Fred.

Once again Joe put on his thinking cap. Looking about him, he quickly made up his mind.

"You see all the straw, floating in the water that Mrs Quack and her ducklings pulled from the horrible scarecrow?" he asked.

"Yes, of course I do," said Fred.

"Get hold of as many pieces as you can and weave them into a rope," said Joe.

The two friends pulled lots of pieces of straw from the water and started to weave them together. Soon, they had a long rope.

JAMIE CLEMENTS aged 9

"Now tie all the boats together with the straw rope and we will pull them all back to Mr Jones," said Joe.

When Mr Jones saw all his boats coming towards him he was absolutely delighted.

"Well done, you two," said Mr Jones.

"Don't forget to thank Mrs Quack and all her family. Without them we could never have done it," said Joe.

That afternoon PC Luca and PC Dragon brought all the boys and girls to the Watery Maze and everyone cheered Joe and Fred for being so clever.

The boys and girls all enjoyed the summer party at the Watery Maze.

And they all lived happily ever after.

JOE AND THE RAILWAY LINE

Once upon a time, in a land far, far away, lived a little boy called Joe. Joe lived with his Mummy and Daddy in a house in the country.

One day, Joe's Mummy asked him if he would like to go to see Mrs Smith who was the station master's wife.

"She hasn't been very well and I thought we could take her a nice cake," said Mummy.

"Will Mr Smith be there?" asked Joe.

"I'm sure he will," said Mummy.

Mummy baked a delicious cake, and when it was time to go to Mrs Smith, they packed the cake in the car, and off they went. The station wasn't too far away and it didn't take very long to get there.

Mummy parked the car. Joe was very helpful because he took the cake for Mummy and walked with her to Mr and Mrs Smith's front door. Mr Smith answered the door and was delighted when he saw not only Mummy, but Joe standing there.

"Come in, come in," he said, "Mrs Smith will be really pleased to see you."

They gave Mr Smith the cake and went up to the bedroom, where Mrs Smith was in bed.

"Just seeing you both has made me feel much better," she said. "While I talk to your Mummy, Joe, why don't you go with Mr Smith to the station to see the trains?"

Joe was only too pleased to go to the station with Mr Smith. As soon as they arrived, Mr Smith showed Joe his enormous map of the railway where you could see all the trains and where they were at any time.

"If you look here Joe, you can see that Tanky is in the goods yard picking up a carriage full of fish and my other engine is in the siding having his wheels cleaned."

Joe was very interested. "Are there any trains expected through the station soon?" he asked.

There should be an express train at ten o'clock. Do you know when it's ten o'clock, Joe?"

"That's when the little hand is on the ten and the big hand is on the twelve" said Joe.

"Exactly," said Mr Smith.

Just then the telephone rang. "Hello," said Mr Smith, "this is the Station Master speaking."

Joe wasn't listening to the phone call until he heard Mr Smith say "oh dear that could be a problem."

"Is there a problem?" asked Joe.

"I think there is," said Mr Smith. "You see, Pressy the Express train is on its way, and that was George the Signalman to tell me that the points are broken, and there may be a crash. The trouble is that Pressy hasn't got a telephone, so I can't call her and I can't think how I can stop her, and I don't know what to do. Can you think of anything, Joe?"

"Now, let me see," said Joe, putting on his thinking cap. He thought long and hard. Suddenly, he looked at Mr Smith and said, "Where did you say Tanky was?"

"He's at the goods yard, picking up a load of fish."

"Has he got a telephone?" asked Joe.

"Why, yes he has," said Mr Smith.

"Then let me call him right away," said Joe.

Quickly, Joe picked up the phone and called Tanky, and then he turned to Mr Smith. "Let's go to platform number one right away, Mr Smith."

The two ran over to platform number one just as Tanky came round the bend, sounding his whistle and as he slowed down, Joe jumped onto his footplate.

"Hang a red lamp in the middle of the track, Mr Smith," said Joe. " Tanky and I will be back as soon as we can; hopefully we will be able to stop Pressy."

Off Tanky raced down the track, with Joe on board.

"What we have to do, Tanky, is to try and stop the express," said Joe.

"I'm not sure if we can do it," said Tanky.

"I've got an idea," said Joe. "Can you slow down just long enough for me to get onto your boiler?"

"Certainly," said Tanky, putting on his brakes.

Joe climbed onto Tanky's boiler. He looked very hard into the distance and that was when he saw Pressy hurtling towards them in a cloud of smoke. Joe started waving his arms and shouting "Stop! Stop."

At first it didn't look as though the express was going to stop, and it went past Tanky and Joe very fast. Joe watched as it went by, and was happy when he saw Pressy the Express slow down and finally stop.

"Back up, quickly, Tanky!" shouted Joe.

When they drew alongside, Pressy was rather cross. "What's the meaning of this?" she said, rather crossly.

Joe explained how the points were broken and Pressy was certainly going to crash. Pressy was really pleased that Joe had made him stop, and said she was sorry for being bad tempered. As the two engines and Joe arrived at the station, Mr Smith was delighted.

"You've really saved the day, Joe," he said, "but before we can all go and have a nice cup of tea, we still have the problem of the broken points."

"Why don't we ask Annabelle to mend them," said Joe.

"Oh you are clever," said Tanky.

So Joe called Annabelle and she agreed to come over and repair the railway points.

"You must come right away," said Joe, "because the points are broken and a train may come along and crash at any time."

"I'll be there as soon as I can," said Annabelle.

Joe waited and waited for Annabelle, but she didn't come.

"I wonder where she can be?" asked Mr Smith.

Just then, Joe heard the sound of flapping wings, and when he looked up, there was Fred the Dragon.

"I'm so glad you've come to see me, Fred," said Joe. "Can you take me on your back and fly over the countryside? We seem to have lost Annabelle, and we need her to mend the railway points."

"Up you get," said Fred.

Joe climbed onto Fred's back, and the two friends flew off over the countryside, in search of Annabelle. They hadn't gone very far, when they saw a long line of cars and trucks, stopped at the side of the road beneath them. There in the middle of the line was Annabelle's truck and at the front of the line was PC Luca in his police car with its lights flashing, and Annabelle was talking to him.

"Let's land please, Fred," Joe said.

They landed right beside PC Luca's car. "We wondered where you had got to, Annabelle," said Joe.

"I'm sorry, Joe," said PC Luca, "but Mr Lion has escaped from the zoo, and until we have caught him we cannot let anyone go along the road."

JAMES LIU aged 8

"What are we going to do?" said PC Luca. "You'd better put on your thinking cap, Joe."

Joe thought and thought. "Is the lion hungry?" he asked.

"Well he hasn't had his lunch yet," said PC Luca.

"We'll be right back," said Joe, and climbed onto Fred's back once again.

"Please would you take me to Mr and Mrs Smith's house, near the station, Fred?" asked Joe.

The two friends flew back to the house, near the station.

"But where is Annabelle? I need the railway points mended before there's a crash," said Mr Smith.

"Don't worry," said Joe, "everything is going to be all right.

Just then, Joe's Mummy came to the front door.

"Is there any of your cake left, Mummy?" Joe asked.

"Yes, I saved quite a big piece for you," she said.

"Please would you give it to me," said Joe.

Mummy went inside Mr and Mrs Smith's house and soon came back with the cake. Joe thanked her, and once again he and Fred flew back to where they had left PC Luca and Annabelle.

"Have you got the Lion's cage ready?" asked Joe.

PC Luca nodded. "All ready Joe," he said.

"Wait there," said Joe, climbing down from Fred's back and walking towards a tree where he could see the lion waiting.

"Are you hungry, Mr Lion?" Joe asked.

"I'm starving," said the lion.

"Well here's some cake for you" said Joe, and he walked back to the cage and placed the cake inside. Mr Lion bounded over, and as soon as he got into the cage to eat the cake, PC Luca closed the door.

"It's now safe for everyone to get on with what they were doing," said PC Luca.

"You'd better hurry to the railway, to mend the points before there's a crash," Joe said to Annabelle, and Annabelle drove off as fast as she could.

"How can I thank you for all that you have done for me?" said Mr Smith.

"Why don't we all go back to your house and have a nice cup of tea!" said Joe.

"That's another good idea you've had," said Mr Smith. "The only thing is that we can't have any cake with the cup of tea."

"Why not?" asked Fred.

"Because Mr Lion ate it!" they all shouted together and everybody laughed.

And they all lived happily ever after.

Mrs Bunn.

JESSICA BOODHUN aged 8

JOE AND THE WALKING TELEPHONE

Once upon a time, in a land far, far away, lived a little boy called Joe. Joe lived with his Mummy and Daddy in a house in the country.

One day, Joe was playing in the garden when he felt very tired. "I know," he thought, "I'll have a quick sleep under my special tree."

Joe lay down under the tree and soon he was fast asleep. He was just having a great dream about eating the biggest slice of chocolate cake, when he heard someone calling his name. Joe opened his eyes and standing in front of him was a telephone, except it wasn't an ordinary phone: this one had arms and legs.

"I'm glad you've woken up Joe," said the telephone. "I was speaking to PC Luca and he told me you were ever so good at solving problems."

"What is the problem?" asked Joe.

"Well, my job is to make sure that people can speak to each other. The trouble is, that a Wicked Witch has cast a spell on all the telephones, and now if you try to call someone you can't get through," said the telephone.

"Is that right?" asked Joe.

"Try now - you try and phone someone on my phone." The telephone handed Joe the handset.

Joe pressed the numbers for Fred the Dragon.

"Hello," said a voice.

"Is that Fred the Dragon?" asked Joe.

"This is Griselda the Wicked Witch," said the voice.

Joe quickly put the phone down.

"I see what you mean, Mr Telephone," he said. "Let me see if I can get through to PC Luca."

Joe dialled the number for PC Luca.

"Hello," said a voice.

MADDIE WRIGHT aged 11

"Is that PC Luca?" asked Joe.

"This is Griselda the Wicked Witch," said the voice.

Joe gave the handset back to the telephone.

"What are we going to do?" asked Mr Telephone.

"I'll have to put on my thinking cap," said Joe.

Joe thought and thought and then smiled; it was the sort of smile when you know that you can make the problem go away. "Right," said Joe, "this is what I want you to do: Can you walk to the tea shop in the village, and ask Mrs Bunn for an enormous chocolate cake?"

"Yes, of course I can," said the walking telephone, "but what is it you are going to do, Joe?" he asked.

"I've got a plan, so you go and get the chocolate cake and I'll see you here in half an hour."

Off went the walking telephone, scratching his mouthpiece, because he could not see how a chocolate cake would help. When the walking telephone got to Mrs Bunn's tea shop, he asked Mrs Bunn for the most enormous cake she could make.

"How big do you want it?" she asked.

"As big as a house," said the walking telephone. Because, being a telephone, he really had no idea how big Joe actually wanted the cake to be.

"As big as a house?" asked Mrs Bunn. "Why, that will take at least three thousand eggs to make it!"

Telephone was a bit worried that he may have asked for a cake that was too big so he telephoned Joe.

"Hello," said a voice.

"Is that Joe?" asked Telephone.

114

"This is Griselda the Wicked Witch," was the reply, and the walking telephone quickly put the phone down. Then he said to Mrs Bunn, that he was happy to have a chocolate cake the size of a house as it was obvious that if Joe had a plan and needed the biggest chocolate cake, then that is what he will have.

When Mrs Bunn told the walking telephone that the cake was ready, the walking telephone was worried that it might be just too big to carry.

"I'll try," he said. Staggering along, the telephone managed to walk all the way to Joe's garden.

"Here it is Joe," said the telephone. "Here's the biggest chocolate cake Mrs Bunn could make."

"That's just what I want," said Joe. "Now we have to find where the Wicked Witch is, so we can put a stop to her horrible plans." Joe wanted to phone his friend Fred the Dragon, but he knew that the Wicked Witch would answer instead. "I know what to do," said Joe.

Joe went out into the garden and asked a pigeon if she would take a message to Dragonland, addressed to Fred.

"Of course I will," said the pigeon. So Joe wrote a note to Fred the Dragon, asking him to come to his house right away.

When Fred received the note he thought it was funny that Joe had not called him on the telephone, so he picked up his phone and dialled Joe's number.

"Hello," said a voice.

"Is that Joe?" asked Fred.

"This is Griselda the Wicked Witch," was the reply. Fred decided to put the phone down and fly as fast as he could to Joe's house.

When he got there, he told Joe all about the telephone call.

"Have you met my friend, the walking telephone?" asked Joe. "He will tell you all about our problem."

The walking telephone told Fred how the Wicked Witch was stopping anyone from speaking on the phone.

"So that was who answered the phone when I called you!" said Fred.

"Exactly," said Joe. "What I want you to do, Fred, is take me on your back and fly over the village to see if we can see where the Wicked Witch lives."

"Get on my back and off we will go," said Fred.

Joe turned to the walking telephone and said, "Will you bring the chocolate cake to wherever we find Griselda?"

"I will," said the walking telephone.

Joe climbed onto Fred's back, and soon they were flying high over the village.

Joe took a special headset out of his pocket and put it over his ears, and listened very carefully.

"Can you fly towards the toy shop please, Fred."

Fred flew over the toy shop, but Joe shook his head. "Nothing there," he said. "Can you fly towards the police station now?" He asked Fred.

Fred and Joe carried on flying in that way. They hadn't gone very far, when Joe heard something on his headset.

"I can hear something coming from that house in the woods, Fred. Can you land nearby?"

Fred landed, and the two friends walked very carefully up to the front door. They listened and they could hear the Wicked Witch inside the house, answering all the telephone calls.

"Right," said Joe, "this is where she is. Will you go and get the walking telephone, and ask him to bring the chocolate cake here as quickly as you can?"

Fred took off and flew back to Joe's house. There, he picked up the walking telephone and the huge chocolate cake and soon he landed back with Joe by the house in the woods.

"Now what I want you to do is cut off a big slice of cake and place it by the back door," said Joe.

As the walking telephone and Fred the Dragon were cutting off a slice of cake, Joe knocked on the door.

"One moment," said a voice, "I'm on the phone."

"Come quickly!" shouted Joe. "I've got something for you!"

No sooner had the Wicked Witch heard Joe than she opened the door and saw the huge slice of cake, taken from the biggest cake ever made.

"Oh, my favourite, I love chocolate cake," said Griselda, and stuffed the huge slice of cake into her mouth.

Just then the telephone rang. "mmm…" said the witch.

"Is that Mrs Bunn?" said a voice.

"Mmm," said Griselda, because you see, her mouth was so full of cake she could not answer, and of course it is rude to speak with your mouth full of food.

When she realised that she couldn't speak, Griselda the Wicked Witch handed the telephone to Joe.

Joe asked the Wicked Witch if she would rather have the delicious cake, or answer all the telephone calls.

"I'd rather have the cake, please," she said.

"Do you promise never to answer the phone again?" asked Joe.

"I promise," said Griselda, her mouth watering with the idea of having such an enormous chocolate cake.

So Joe gave her the chocolate cake, and Fred and Joe flew back to Joe's house, where the walking telephone was waiting for them.

"From now on, all telephone calls will be all right," said Joe.

"Oh, thank you," said the walking telephone.

From that day on, the Wicked Witch was so happy eating her chocolate cake that she never ever answered the phone again.

And they all lived happily ever after.

ASHLEY CLYNES aged 8

JOE AND THE WALLPAPER

Once upon a time, in a land far, far away, lived a little boy called Joe. Joe lived with his Mummy and Daddy in a house in the country.

One day, Joe was getting ready for bed. He said good night to his Mummy and Daddy. He climbed into bed and closed his eyes.

"What a lovely day I had today at Lavender Farm," he thought. Then he smiled, because he remembered that the next day, he was going to visit his friend, Fred the Dragon in Dragonland.

"I must get up early," he said to himself; at least he thought it was to himself but someone said, "what time would you like me to wake you up Joe?"

"Who said that?" asked Joe.

"Me," said the voice, and as Joe looked, the whole of his room lit up with a lovely blue light, and the walls started to glow.

"It's me, the wallpaper," said the voice.

Joe was surprised.

"I've never heard of wallpaper talking before," said Joe.

"That's because the decorator bought me in a magic shop," said the wallpaper.

"Can you really wake me up whenever I want?" asked Joe.

"Of course I can," said the wallpaper. "I'd hardly be magic if I couldn't do something like that now, would I?"

"What else can you do?" asked Joe.

"Would you like to see?" the wallpaper said.

"Yes please," said Joe.

"Then watch the wall very closely." As the wallpaper spoke, the whole wall turned into a giant television screen.

Joe was amazed to see himself riding on Louise the tractor at Lavender Farm.

"Why that's me," he said "It's like watching what I did today, all over again."

"Yes," said Wallpaper, "is there anything else that you would like to see?"

Joe thought and thought and then smiled as he remembered what he most wanted.

"Can you show me where all the toys that Father Christmas makes come from? You see, I would like to ask him for a new train set and don't know his address."

"I can do better than that," said the wallpaper. "If you get out of bed and come over here and close your eyes, I'll take you there."

No sooner had Joe walked over to the wallpaper, than he felt himself flying through the air. He flew over his village and on over Dragonland, and soon he was flying over the North Pole.

"Wow," he thought, "this is exciting."

In the middle of the North Pole, he felt himself slowing down and, as he landed, he saw a lovely house almost hidden in the snow. Joe walked over to the house and heard tapping and banging coming from inside. Joe knocked on the door and waited. Soon the door opened and there was a little Elf.

"Hello," said Joe, "my name is..."

The little Elf started to laugh. He laughed and laughed until the tears ran down his face.

"Why are you laughing?" asked Joe.

"Why your name is Joe," said the little Elf. "At Father Christmas's house, we know the name of all the boys and girls. Now, how can I help you, Joe?"

"I've come to see Father Christmas," said Joe. "At least, my friend, the wallpaper has flown me here to see him, if that's all right?"

The little Elf looked very sad.

"What's the matter?" asked Joe.

"I'm afraid we've lost him," said the Elf.

"Lost him?" said Joe. "Lost father Christmas?"

"The problem is, he went out in the snow last night and didn't take any of his reindeer, and we think he may have got lost," said the Elf.

"Can I help you find him?" asked Joe.

"I was hoping you would say that," said the elf. "Everyone in Toyland has heard how clever you are at finding people."

"I'll put on my thinking cap and see what I can do," said Joe.

Joe thought and thought, and then had a brilliant idea.

"I don't have to think; I'll ask my friend, the wallpaper to help. Are you there?" he asked out loud.

"I'm here," said a voice." What do you want, Joe?"

"Father Christmas is lost and the elves don't know where he is. Can you use your magic powers and help me find him please?"

"Of course I can," said the wallpaper. "Close your eyes and we can start."

Joe closed his eyes and, once again, he found himself flying through the air.

This time they hadn't gone very far when Joe, opening his eyes, shouted, "I can see something red in the snow down below!"

As he landed, he saw that the something red was Father Christmas's jacket.

"I wonder where he can be?" thought Joe. "After all, it's very cold at the North Pole, and I wouldn't like Father Christmas to catch a cold, without his jacket."

Joe walked along in the snow and heard someone cry out.

"Help! Help!" he heard.

"I'm coming," said Joe, and he raced to where he heard the cry for help. Joe arrived at a big hole in the ground. When he looked into the hole, there was Father Christmas lying at the very bottom.

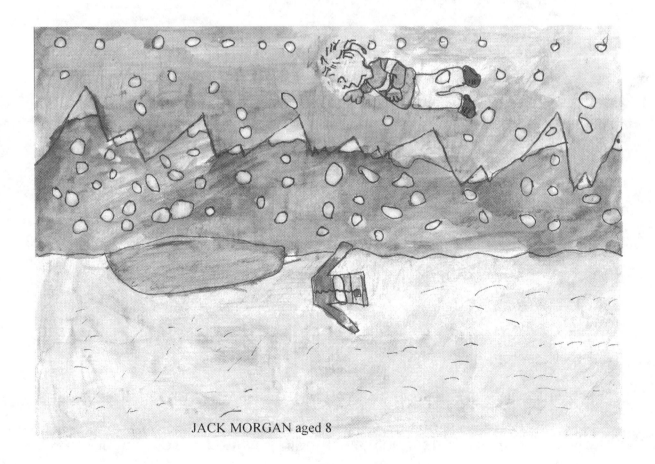

JACK MORGAN aged 8

123

"Are you all right down there?" asked Joe.

"I think so," said Father Christmas. "The problem is, I don't think I can climb out of the hole by myself, as it is too steep."

"Leave it to me," said Joe.

"Can you fly me back to Father Christmas's house, please, wallpaper?" He said.

"Close your eyes again," said the wallpaper and, once again, Joe felt himself flying through the air.

Joe landed at the house and knocked on the door. When the elf opened it, Joe explained how he had found Father Christmas and how he had fallen into a big hole.

"Whatever are we to do?" asked the Elf.

"What I need are two reindeer and a long piece of rope," said Joe.

The Elf took Joe around to the back of Father Christmas's house and let Joe have two reindeers from the stable. "And here is an extra long rope," said the elf.

Joe climbed onto the back of one of the reindeers and soon they were flying again. This time Joe was flying because Father Christmas's reindeers are also magic animals, and can fly through the air, just like birds.

Joe soon found the hole again and shouted down to Father Christmas. "I'm throwing down a rope; hold on to it and we will soon pull you out."

So saying, Joe tied one end of the rope to the two reindeers and dropped the other end down the hole.

"Hold tight," said Joe, and told the reindeers to walk backwards. As the reindeers walked, they pulled Father Christmas right out of the deep hole. When Father Christmas was standing by the side of him, Joe gave him back his jacket.

"How can I ever thank you, Joe?" Father Christmas said. "I took off my jacket so that someone might find me, because it is so red and shiny, but then I fell into the hole and didn't think that anyone would ever rescue me."

"You're very welcome," said Joe.

"What would you like as a reward?" asked Father Christmas.

"I don't need a reward for a good deed," said Joe, but I was rather hoping to get a new train set. I know I will have to wait until Christmas for it, but that's what I would really like to have."

"I'll have to see what I can do," said Father Christmas. "Now let's get back to my house and have a nice hot drink to warm ourselves, shall we?"

"That would be great," said Joe.

When all the Elves saw Father Christmas had been found, they were delighted and they all thanked Joe for being so clever.

NADINE ATKIN aged 8

"Don't thank me," said Joe, "thank the wallpaper."

"Wallpaper? We can't see any wallpaper," everyone said together.

"It's magic wallpaper and…" Joe stopped and smiled. "Of course you can't see the wallpaper, it's back in my room."

"Well, I don't know about you, Joe, but I'm cold and I would like to have a hot drink," said Father Christmas.

The Elves all rushed around and soon they had made a lovely hot cup of tea with a huge chocolate cake. When Joe had finished his tea, he said that he had better be going, because he hadn't gone to sleep yet and he was very tired. He said goodbye to Father Christmas and all the elves.

"I'm ready to go home now, wallpaper," he said.

"Close your eyes," said the wallpaper.

Once again, Joe felt himself flying through the air. When Joe opened his eyes, he was in bed and it was morning. The wallpaper certainly was not lit up. In fact it looked like any wallpaper that you see anywhere.

"It must all have been a dream," he thought.

Just then, Mummy and Daddy called for him to come down for breakfast.

As Joe got out of bed, something dug into his foot, and when he looked down, there on the floor was the biggest train set you have ever seen.

"Well, fancy that," said Joe and he smiled. He knew who had given him the train set and where it had come from, and of course, how it had got there, even though it was not Christmas.

And they all lived happily ever after.

BETHANY BANNISTER aged 8

JOE AND THE MAGIC WAND

Once upon a time, in a land far, far away, lived a little boy called Joe. Joe lived with his Mummy and Daddy in a house in the country.

One day, Joe was in bed fast asleep, when he thought he heard his Mummy call to him that she could hear the postman coming up the path. Sleepily, Joe went down the stairs to the front door. As he got there, the letter box opened and a huge envelope came through it.

"Thank you," said Joe to Bill the Postman, through the door.

"You're welcome, Joe," said Bill, as he went off to the house next door.

Joe picked up the huge envelope and opened it, and there inside was a huge card; on it, written in huge letters, was an invitation to Fred the Dragon's birthday party. The party was to be on the following Sunday, in Dragonland.

"May I go please, Mummy?" Joe asked.

"Of course you can," she said.

"Will you please take me to buy a birthday present for Fred today? Joe asked.

"When we go shopping this afternoon, we can get one then," said Mummy.

That afternoon, Mummy and Daddy took Joe with them when they went shopping.

"What would you like to buy Fred?" asked Daddy.

"I'm going to buy him a magic wand," said Joe. "I think he wants one, because whenever I get my wand out he gets excited and I'm sure he would like to have one of his own."

CHARLOTTE GARCIA aged 9

129

"We'll stop off at the magic shop then," said Daddy.

Off they all went to the high street, and when they got to the magic shop, Mummy and Daddy decided to leave Joe with Uncle Sam, the Magician.

"We'll be back at six o'clock," said Daddy. "That's when the little hand is on the six and the big hand is on the twelve.

"I know that," said Joe, "and I'll be ready; see you then. Bye!"

"Bye, Joe," said Mummy and Daddy.

Joe stood in front of the magic shop. As he stood there, the front door opened and Joe smiled, because he knew that, as this was a magic shop, everything happened by magic. He went inside and there was a very kindly man, standing there.

"Hello, Joe," said the man.

"Hello, Uncle Sam," said Joe.

"I haven't seen you since you came to buy your magic wand," said Uncle Sam. "What can I do for you today?"

"I've come to buy a magic wand for my best friend, Fred the Dragon," said Joe.

Uncle Sam looked very sad.

"Whatever is the matter?" asked Joe.

"I'm afraid I haven't got any wands in the shop," said Uncle Sam. "You see, in order to make a wand magic, it has to have a piece of a wish bone; now the wish bone comes from a chicken, and the chickens come from Billy the Butcher, but Billy is on his holiday and won't be back for a long time. Until he comes back, I can't make any magic wands. I'm sorry Joe."

Joe put on his thinking cap.

"What do you want to do, Joe?" asked Uncle Sam. "Whenever you put on your thinking cap, I know you're going to come up with a very clever answer."

"Well, I've brought my magic wand with me, so if I use it, I should be able to find Billy the Butcher wherever he is on holiday, and see if he can find a wish bone for Fred's wand."

"Good idea," said Uncle Sam.

Joe brought his magic wand out of his pocket. "Abracadabra," he said.

All of a sudden, with a flash and a bang, Joe found himself on a desert island, right outside a tent.

"Hello," said a deep voice, "who are you and how did you get here?"

"I'm Joe and I'm looking for Billy the Butcher."

"Oh! I'm Willy the Watcher," said the voice.

"I must have said the wrong spell," said Joe and said goodbye to Willy the Watcher.

Joe waved his wand again and this time, after the usual flash and bang, Joe found himself in a car driving along a country road. Inside the car, was Billy the Butcher.

"Who are you?" asked Billy.

"I'm Joe and I've come to ask if you can let me have a wishbone for Fred the Dragon's new wand."

Billy stopped the car and turned to Joe. "I'm on my holiday, Joe, and I haven't brought any wishbones with me," said Billy.

"Ah, but you will know where to get them, won't you?" asked Joe.

"Of course. If you go to the farmer at the end of the field over there," said Billy, pointing to a farmhouse on the nearby hill, "tell the farmer, I sent you, and ask him to give you a wishbone."

HANNAH STEAD aged 10

"Thank you," said Joe.

Billy drove off leaving Joe at the side of the road. Joe walked up the road, but never seemed to get any closer to the farmhouse on the hill.

"That's funny," he thought, "every time I try to walk along the road, I seem to slip back to where I started."

Joe looked down and saw a green liquid all over the road. "Whatever is that?" thought Joe. Just then, he heard someone whistling. The whistling sound came from the other side of a fence at the side of the road. When Joe looked, who do you think he saw? It was Annabelle.

"Hello, Annabelle, fancy seeing you here," said Joe.

"Hello, Joe," said Annabelle. "Yes, I'm building a new laundry for Mrs Smith, the farmer's wife."

And that was when Joe smiled again. "Tell me, Annabelle, what did you do with the old washing machine when you started to build the laundry?"

"I put it at the side of the road for me to load onto my truck later," said Annabelle.

"Well that was very naughty," said Joe. "All the old washing liquid from it has spread all over the road, and now you can't walk along without slipping backwards."

"Oh dear," said Annabelle, "I am sorry. I shall clear it up right away."

Annabelle climbed over the fence to where Joe was standing and cleared up the washing liquid. When it was all gone, Joe tried to move and was pleased that he could now walk along the road, without slipping backwards.

"But why are you here?" asked Annabelle as they walked along together.

"I'm on my way to get a wishbone for Fred the Dragon's wand from the farmer," Said Joe. "I'll give the wand to Fred at his birthday party."

"Of course, I'm going to Fred's party as well," said Annabelle. "Why don't I come along with you?"

Off the two went and soon came to the farmhouse, and when Joe explained what he wanted, the farmer was only too delighted to help.

"Here you are, Joe," he said, as he handed Joe a very nice wishbone.

"Thank you," said Joe.

"See you at the party, Annabelle, "said Joe, as he waved his magic wand and arrived back at the magic shop.

"Did you get it?" asked Uncle Sam.

"Here it is," said Joe, placing the wishbone in front of Uncle Sam.

Uncle Sam went to the back of the shop with the wishbone and came back holding a beautiful new magic wand.

"Here you are, Joe, I think this must be one of the best wands I have ever made."

"Thank you, Uncle Sam," said Joe.

Taking the new wand Joe went outside, and because Mummy and Daddy hadn't come along yet, because it wasn't six o'clock, Joe fell asleep under a tree. It seemed to Joe that he hadn't been asleep very long when he heard someone saying, "Wake up, Joe, wake up!"

Joe woke up in his bed at home. He'd been dreaming after all, and then he remembered that it was Fred the Dragon's party today and he had already bought Fred a lovely new wand.

And they all lived happily ever after.

MOLLIE CATLIN aged 10

JOE AND THE UNICORN

Once upon a time, in a land far, far away, lived a little boy called Joe. Joe lived with his Mummy and Daddy in a house in the country.

One day, Joe was invited to his friend, Fred the Dragon. After they had had lunch, Fred suggested that they could go to the Watery Maze, to see if they could find the treasure.

"Is there really treasure at the Watery Maze, Fred?" Joe asked.

"Everyone talks about it," said Fred.

"Then let's go there!" said Joe.

Off went the two friends.

When they arrived at the Watery Maze, they wanted to buy a treasure map from Mr Jones, the man who was in charge, but Mr Jones remembered how helpful they had been in rescuing all his boats from the horrible scarecrow and gave them the map free of charge, saying, "I must warn you, Joe, the scarecrows are back, so do be careful."

"We will," said Joe, and he thanked Mr Jones.

When Fred the Dragon opened the map Joe said, "I expect we have to go to the centre of the maze - what do you think, Fred?"

"Let's go," said Fred.

They hadn't gone very far, when they met a unicorn. "Hello," said the unicorn, "my name is Uni and I shall be your guide around the maze today."

"How do you do," said the two friends, very politely.

"Can you help us find the treasure please?" asked Joe.

CHRISTOPHER HORT aged 7

"Of course I can," said Uni .

Off they all went and when they came to the Watery Maze, they all got in a boat. Uni looked at his map and said, "I think we have to go this way," pointing to a long watery pathway." There are only ten dead ends before we get to the middle, so we must be careful to count them or we will get lost. Better let me do the counting!"

They passed by the first dead end and the unicorn counted, number one.

They hadn't gone very far when they saw another unicorn, but this one was really a nasty unicorn.

"Why don't you go up that watery pathway?" the nasty unicorn suggested.

The friends turned the boat and rowed up the way that the nasty unicorn mentioned.

That's funny ,"said Uni, the nice unicorn, "I am the guide here at the Watery Maze, but I don't remember going this way before."

Joe kept rowing up the strange watery pathway. As they turned a corner there were two horrible scarecrows. When the scarecrows saw the friends they shouted and quickly climbed into their scarecrow boats to chase Joe and his friends.

"I told you I didn't like the look of that dead end," said Uni.

Joe rowed as fast as he could go and soon the horrible scarecrows were nowhere to be seen.

"Hello again," said a voice, and when they looked over to the side of the maze, there was the nasty unicorn.

"We're not going to take any more advice from you," said Fred the Dragon. "The last direction you gave us nearly got us captured by two horrible scarecrows."

"Well, I don't mean to be nasty, Fred," said the nasty unicorn, "it's just that my unicorn horn has got bent and it's made me nasty. If only I could get it straightened out, I'm sure I would be as nice as pie."

"What's your name?" asked Joe.

"My name is Twitchy," said the nasty unicorn.

"Well, why don't you come along with us," said Joe, "and when we find the treasure we will have enough money to send you to have your horn straightened."

"Oh, thank you, Joe," said Twitchy, and he got into the boat.

"Better be quick," said Uni. "The scarecrows are catching up."

Sure enough, Joe could see that there were now ten scarecrows after them.

"They've brought all their friends along, by the look of it," said Joe.

"Better row as fast as you can and try to get away," said Fred, and that is exactly what Joe did.

When they went past the very next dead end, Twitchy shouted. "That's number three: Only seven more to go, then we will be at the centre of the maze, and I'm sure that's where you will find the treasure."

But as fast as they went the scarecrows seemed to be catching up with them.

"Now, come on Joe," Fred said, "where's your thinking cap? We need to get out of trouble."

Joe thought and thought and then smiled his special smile for whenever he had a good idea.

"Let's steer over there!" Joe said, pointing to where there were a lot of rocks sticking out of the water.

"But we won't be able to pass through there," said Uni. "There isn't much water and there are lots of rocks sticking up."

"Don't you worry," said Joe, and carried on heading straight for where it looked very dangerous.

Joe, Fred, Uni and Twitchy all watched closely as the ten horrible scarecrows followed them into the dangerous place.

Just as Joe steered them out of danger, they heard a cry and when they looked, the boat with the ten scarecrows was sinking.

"Their boat is sinking," shouted Fred, "and we came through all right! How did you know it would happen?" he asked Joe.

"Well you see," said Joe, "there are only four of us, and so we were not as heavy as the other boat which had ten horrible scarecrows in it. Because they were so heavy, they hit all the rocks under the boat, and they will never be a problem again."

Joe then carried on rowing along the Watery Maze...

"There goes number seven," said Uni. "Only three more to go!"

They hadn't gone much further, when they came across a huge ship, anchored in the middle of the watery pathway.

"What a big ship!" said Fred "Who does that belong to?"

"All I know is that it came along yesterday, and no one knows anything about it," said Twitchy.

Just then, they heard shouting coming from the ship...

"What's all that shouting?" asked Uni.

"Let's go and see," said Joe, rowing towards the back of the ship.

When they got there, they could hear a lot of people singing.

"We're here to find the treasure," they all sang together.

"I know who they are," said Joe. "They are pirates and they have come to find the treasure before we find it."

"What can we do?" asked Twitchy. "We've only just got rid of the horrible scarecrows, and now we have this problem.

"Can you put on your thinking cap again please, Joe?" asked Uni.

Once again Joe thought and thought. Then the old smile crossed his face and Fred knew that Joe had had another one of his brilliant ideas.

"Has anyone got a piece of paper and a pencil?" Joe asked.

"Here you are, Joe," said Fred, "I always carry a piece of paper and a pencil, just in case I have any ideas that I need to write down."

Fred gave Joe his piece of paper and his pencil, and at once Joe started to draw and write things on the paper. He took quite a while and then, when he was finished, he held it up for his friends to see.

ALYSSA YAP YOUNG aged 8

"Why, it looks exactly like a treasure map," said Fred.

"That's just what it is," said Joe. "Now all we have to do is get this piece of paper on board the pirate ship."

"Leave that to me," said Twitchy. "After all, I was rather nasty to you before, and I need to make it up to you."

Twitchy took the paper and asked Joe to row to the side of the ship, which of course Joe, was delighted to do. When they got to the side of the ship, Twitchy placed Joe's drawing on his bent unicorn horn and moved his horn into place around the nearest canon. When he was sure that no one was watching, Twitchy let go of the paper, and it stayed lying on the deck of the ship.

"We can go now," Twitchy said to Joe, and Joe rowed to the bank to hide in the reeds at the side of the maze.

They didn't have to wait very long; the ship started to move and soon had disappeared around the bend in the watery pathway.

"Whatever did you put on the map that Twitchy left for the pirates?" asked Fred.

Joe laughed. "The map showed that the treasure was in a completely different place and it will take them weeks before they find out that we have tricked them," he said. "Come on we had better keep rowing, or we will never find the treasure for ourselves."

Soon, Joe was rowing along the Watery Maze again.

"We've just gone past dead end number ten, so we should see the middle of the maze very soon, and that's where the treasure is buried" Said Uni.

As they turned the corner, there was a huge island.

"Do you think the treasure could be buried on that island?" asked Fred.

"Only one way to find out," said Joe, and rowed for all he was worth towards the island.

"Better get out the real treasure map," Joe said, and Fred spread it out for them all to see.

"I think the treasure is buried there," said Uni, pointing to a big cross on the ground.

"We can't dig for it," said Fred. "We haven't got anything to dig with."

"Oh yes we have," said Twitchy, and started to dig with his unicorn horn. "Come on Uni, use your horn as well."

Very soon the two unicorns had made a great big hole, and sure enough, there was a big chest under all the sand that they had dug up.

"Better stop there," said Joe, and he bent down and opened the chest. Inside was a huge treasure.

When they took the treasure to Mr Jones, he was delighted and agreed to give enough money to Twitchy to have his horn straightened.

Everyone was happy that they had lots of treasure.

And they all lived happily ever after.

JOE AND THE WITCH

Once upon a time, in a land far, far away, lived a little boy called Joe. Joe lived with his Mummy and Daddy in a house in the country.

One day, one snowy day when it was snowing, Joe asked his Mummy and Daddy if he could call his friend, Fred the Dragon. Joe asked Fred if he would like to play with him on his sledge and slide along on the snow.

"I'd love to! I'll fly right over now!" said Fred.

When he arrived, Joe's Mummy and Daddy made sure that they were both wrapped up in nice warm clothes.

"Be careful to keep to the path, won't you, Joe," Mummy said.

Joe went into the garage and found his sledge. He took it off the shelf where it had been since last winter and went outside to find Fred. Soon, the two friends were having so much fun that they forgot what Mummy had told them. They played along the path only for a while, but the snow was better near the forest, and that was where they went.

It wasn't long before the two friends found themselves in the middle of the dark forest.

"Oh dear," said Fred, "I hope we're not lost!"

"We may be," said Joe. "I don't recognise anything at all."

They went further along the path, pulling the sledge along and it wasn't long before Joe had to admit that they were probably lost after all.

"Look over there!" said Fred. "There's a cottage!"

"Maybe we can ask the person who lives there, the way back to our home," said Joe.

DANIEL DAVIES-GOMEZ aged 8

They knocked on the door, and a voice said, "Who is it?"

"It's me," said Joe.

"Me? Who's me?" said the voice.

"It's Joe," he said.

"One minute then, Joe," said the voice, and Joe and Fred waited by the door.

After a few minutes the door opened, and there was an old lady.

"Good afternoon," said Joe, "we seem to be lost and would like to know the way home: Can you help us please?"

"Why don't you come in for a while,?" said the old lady.

Now, Joe and Fred didn't know that the old lady was a wicked old witch and they agreed to go into her house.

"Would you like to have a nice cup of tea?" The Wicked Witch asked.

"Yes please," said Fred the Dragon, because dragons are always thirsty on account of all the hot air they breathe out.

"Make yourselves at home," said the Wicked Witch. And because Joe and Fred didn't know who she was, they sat down on the sofa. The Wicked Witch made a pot of tea and poured out two cups.

"Aren't you having any tea?" asked Fred.

"I had my tea an hour ago," said the Wicked Witch, and she poured out two cups, one for Fred and one for Joe.

"It tastes a bit strange," said Joe.

"That's because it's made from special herbs," said the Wicked Witch. "Now drink it all up!"

Joe and Fred drank their tea, and afterwards the two friends started to yawn.

"I think we'd better leave before we go to sleep," said Joe, but when he tried to get up he felt as though he wanted to sleep there and then. Soon, both Fred and Joe fell fast asleep.

The Wicked Witch said, "Ho ho, those two have gone to sleep and now I can cast a magic spell and turn them into cats!"

"Abracadabra!" she said, and waved her hand at Fred.

With a huge bang, Fred immediately turned into a cat, but the bang woke Joe up. When he saw what the Wicked Witch had done, Joe ran out of the house, and seeing his sledge at the side of the house, climbed on to it and slid up the path as quickly as he could. Luckily he went the right way, and soon he found himself out of the forest and very near the police station.

"Thank goodness," he thought. "I must get PC Luca to help me rescue my friend, Fred the Dragon."

Joe knocked on the police station door and when PC Luca opened it, Joe told him all about the Wicked Witch and how she had turned Fred into a cat.

"What we have to do," said PC Luca, "is go back into the forest and find the Wicked Witch's house and see if we can find a magic spell to change Fred back again."

The two friends set out, and soon they entered the forest. After a while they came to a clearing, and there in the middle was the Wicked Witch's house.

"What shall we do now?" asked PC Luca.

"Why don't we stand either side of the door and when the Wicked Witch answers the door we can get hold of her and make sure she can't do any magic," said Joe.

Sure enough when they knocked on the door, the Wicked Witch said, "Hello who is there?"

LILY SEWELL aged 8

"It's me!" said PC Luca.

"Who is me?" asked the Wicked Witch.

"Luca," he said, thinking he had better not say PC Luca, because he did not want to tell the Wicked Witch that he was a policeman.

The witch opened the door, and PC Luca grabbed her and put his handcuffs on her wrists so she couldn't move. As soon as the Wicked Witch was handcuffed, Joe went into the Wicked Witch's house and found her magic spell book, and turned to the page that said how to turn people back into what they should be.

He looked around for Fred, but he was nowhere to be seen.

"What are we going to do?" asked PC Luca. "After all, if we can't find him, Fred will have to be a cat forever and ever."

Joe put on his thinking cap and slowly an idea came to him.

"Let's go into the kitchen and find the fridge!" Joe said to PC Luca.

"The kitchen? The fridge? We're trying to find Fred the Dragon, and you want to find the fridge? Do you know what you are doing, Joe?" PC Luca asked.

"Don't worry," said Joe crossing the room and going into the kitchen.

While PC Luca stood, scratching his head wondering what his friend was doing, Joe went to a cupboard and took out a bowl, and then he opened the fridge and took out a bottle of milk. Joe poured some milk into the bowl and put it down on the floor. PC Luca still didn't know what Joe was going to do next, but when Joe said, "Here kitty, kitty," PC Luca realised just what Joe was doing.

Once again, Joe called even louder, "Here kitty, kitty!"

All of a sudden there was the sound of a cat, "Meow, meow," it went, and then Fred the cat came into the room.

"Abracadabra!" said Joe.

With a loud bang, Fred found himself turned back into his old self.

"Thank you," said Fred.

"That was really clever, Joe," said PC Luca. But what are we to do with the Wicked Witch?" He asked. "Do you think I should take her back to the police station?"

"I've got a better idea," said Joe. "Wait there a moment!"

Joe walked back into the Wicked Witch's living room and picked up her book of spells. But outside the house, the Wicked Witch had managed to wriggle out of the handcuffs.

"I can't wait to turn those three into sausages!" she said.

She opened the door just as Joe turned to the page of the spell book that said 'how to make nasty people nice'.

The witch took one look at the three friends and pointing to them said, "Become sausa…"

But before she could say the whole word, sausages, Joe shouted, "Abracadabra!"

Then a funny thing happened: The witch's black clothes turned pink, and her nasty face became beautiful, and she turned to the three friends and said, "Would anyone like a cup of nice tea?"

And remembering what happened the last time they had a drink in the witch's house, Joe and Fred shouted "NO THANK YOU!"

"Oh, it won't be a nasty cup of tea," said the now Beautiful Witch. "There will be lovely sandwiches and chocolate cake."

"Oh that's different!" said Joe, because he could see that the Wicked Witch was now a really nice person.

And they all lived happily ever after.

JOE AND SAMUEL FUZZYHEAD

Once upon a time, in a land far, far away, lived a little boy called Joe. Joe lived with his Mummy and Daddy in a house in the country.

One day, Joe's Mummy asked him if he could go to the shops and buy some eggs, so that she could make Joe and his Daddy a lovely cake.

"Be sure to come right home," said his Mummy, "because I would like to bake the cake in time for tea".

"Of course I will," said Joe.

Mummy gave Joe some money, and off he went to the shops. On his way, Joe saw a sign; it said Cleverland, this way to the shops. "That's clever," thought Joe, "Nice of them to tell me the way."

He crossed over the road and followed the sign to the shops. When he got there, there was a long queue of people outside the shop that sold eggs.

"What shall I do?" said Joe. "I have to be home soon, because Mummy is waiting for the eggs to make a cake, and this queue of people could take a long time to get served."

"Can I help?" said a voice behind him.

Joe turned around and was delighted to see his old friend, PC Luca.

"I don't know if you can, PC Luca. Mummy wants some eggs to make a cake and needs to bake it in time for our tea, but this queue of people is so long, I don't think I will be back in time."

"Why don't I take you in my police car to Mrs Chicken, to buy some eggs from her, because after all that's where they come from in the first place," said PC Luca.

"That would be good," said Joe. "And how clever of you to think of that."

"They don't call this Cleverland for nothing you know," said PC Luca, laughing.

Joe got into the police car and PC Luca suggested that, as it was nearly an emergency, he might use his siren to get to Mrs Chicken very quickly. Joe had always wanted to travel in a police car with the siren blasting away, and happily agreed to it.

Off they went, with the siren making an enormous noise. They hadn't gone very far when there, in the middle of the road, was a little round man, waving at them. PC Luca screeched his police car to a stop.

"Who is that little man?" said Joe. "And why is he waving at us from the middle of the road when he could so easily get hurt?"

"Well, you know we are in Cleverland," said PC Luca, "and you know who lives there, who does not quite fit in?"

"Of course, it's Samuel Fuzzyhead," said Joe.

"Exactly!" said PC Luca. "The trouble is, Samuel Fuzzyhead is far from being clever and always gets into a muddle whenever he tries. I expect he's trying to be clever now. Let's see what he wants, shall we, Joe?"

The two friends got out of the police car.

"What's the matter, Samuel Fuzzyhead?" asked Joe. "And why are you standing in the middle of the road, waving your arms at us?"

"Was I?" said Samuel Fuzzyhead. "Now let me think; why was I waving?"

Samuel Fuzzyhead thought and thought. "I remember! I want to go to see Mrs Chicken to get some milk," he said.

"You can't do that," said Joe.

"Why not?" said Samuel Fuzzyhead.

"You are silly, Samuel Fuzzyhead; Mrs Chicken doesn't sell milk, she sells eggs," said PC Luca.

ADAM MOUNTNEY aged 8

"Oh yes, I forgot," said Samuel Fuzzyhead. Then he stopped and thought and turned to Joe.

"Do you think I'm silly, Joe?"

"Of course not! I think you are being a little forgetful, that's all. Why don't you get into the police car with us and we can take you to Lavender Farm. It's on the way and you can ask Mrs Cow for some milk."

"Oh, thank you, Joe" said Samuel Fuzzyhead and then he stopped and thought again.

"Now what's wrong?" asked PC Luca.

"I can't remember if I wanted to get some milk from Mrs Cow or some eggs from Mrs Chicken," said Samuel Fuzzyhead.

"What shall we do?" said PC Luca.

"We'll have to think about it," said Joe. "In the meantime, let's get into the police car."

Off they all went, in the police car. They hadn't gone very far when they saw Fred the Dragon talking to Annabelle.

"Hello," shouted Joe, "I didn't know you visited Cleverland."

"We're on our way to buy some carrots from Farmer Jones," said Annabelle.

"Are they for your supper?" asked Joe.

"Actually, they are to squeeze out and make a carrot coloured paint for Fred the Dragon's new play room," said Annabelle.

"Why not get into the police car and I'll drive you there?" said PC Luca.

So off went Samuel Fuzzyhead, Annabelle, Fred the Dragon, PC Luca and Joe, all packed inside the little police car. They hadn't gone very far, when a voice cried out, "I've got it!" It was Samuel Fuzzyhead.

"What have you got?" asked Joe.

"You know that I couldn't remember whether to buy eggs from Mrs Chicken or milk from Mrs Cow?"

"Yes," said Joe.

"I know the answer," said Samuel Fuzzyhead.

"And what is the answer?" asked Joe.

"Why, I shall buy both! I'll get some milk from Mrs Cow and eggs from Mrs Chicken."

"That is clever," said Joe.

Samuel Fuzzyhead beamed all over.

"Do you really think I'm clever, Joe?" asked Samuel Fuzzyhead.

"It's by far the cleverest thing I've heard all day," said Joe.

Samuel Fuzzyhead glowed with pride. "You've made me very happy, Joe;

now I can live in Cleverland and know that I am as clever as everyone else. Thank you."

For the rest of the journey he sat and giggled, all the way to Farmer Jones's.

When at last Fred the Dragon and Annabelle had bought their carrots and they had gone on to Mrs Cow for Samuel Fuzzyhead to buy some milk, they arrived at Mrs Chicken to find that she was not at home.

"Look at the time!" said PC Luca. "The big hand is on the twelve and the little hand is on the three."

"It's three o'clock!" said Joe. "However am I going to be able to get back to Mummy in time for her to bake a cake for tea?"

"I've got an idea," said Samuel Fuzzyhead. "Why don't you call Mrs Chicken on her telephone?"

"You are so clever," said Joe, and once again Samuel Fuzzyhead beamed with pleasure.

Quickly, Joe dialled the number, and asked if Mrs Chicken could hurry back to sell him some eggs.

"I'm on my way," she said, and appeared from around the back of her house. "I was there all the time!" she laughed. "How many eggs would you like?"

"Six please, Mrs Chicken," said Joe, and Mrs Chicken counted them out.

"And I would like the same as Joe please, Mrs Chicken," said Samuel Fuzzyhead.

Samuel looked at Joe, who was looking very worried.

"Whatever is the matter?" asked Samuel Fuzzyhead.

"Now, how am I ever going to get back in time? It's very late," said Joe.

155

"Why don't you ask Fred the Dragon to fly you home?" said Samuel.

"That is quite brilliant," said Joe.

And Samuel Fuzzyhead beamed with pleasure.

So Joe climbed up onto Fred the Dragon's back and waved goodbye to PC Luca and Annabelle and of course, his new and very clever friend, Samuel Fuzzyhead. Soon, Fred and Joe were high up in the sky over his house. Joe's Mummy was a bit cross when Joe arrived late, but when Joe told her about his adventure, Mummy was very pleased with him for being so kind to Samuel Fuzzyhead.

"After all," she said "we must always try to be nice and help people, mustn't we?"

Mummy made a lovely cake and when Daddy arrived home they all sat down to a magnificent tea.

And they all lived happily ever after.

JOE AND THE TALKING FOOTBALL

Once upon a time, in a land far, far away, lived a little boy called Joe. Joe lived with his Mummy and Daddy in a house in the country.

One day, Joe decided to have a barbeque and he invited all his friends. The first to arrive was his special friend, Fred the Dragon. Now you may know that all dragons can breathe fire and hot air, and Joe being very clever had asked Fred to come early so that he could breathe fire on his barbeque to get it started.

Sure enough, Fred breathed on the charcoal and soon it was burning very nicely. The next to arrive was Annabelle, who used all her tools to build some lovely chairs and tables for everyone to sit down to eat.

All the other friends arrived but the one person missing was PC Luca. Soon, they all heard a police siren and PC Luca arrived.

"Now that everyone is here, let's eat!" said Joe.

Everybody sat down and tucked into the lovely food.

When they had all eaten, Fred the Dragon said, "I feel so full, I think I need something to make the food go down."

"Why don't we all play football?" said PC Luca.

"Great idea!" everyone said together.

So Joe went to his room to find his football. He opened his toy box and there inside was his football. As Joe lifted the football out of his toy box he was amazed to see that it was crying.

"Whatever is the matter?" asked Joe.

"I'm so sad," said the football. "I seem to spend all my time in the toy box, and no one wants to play with me."

"Well, you're wanted now," said Joe.

"Am I really?" asked the football.

"Yes, come on, everyone's waiting to play with you." And Joe picked up the football and took him out to the garden.

Everybody enjoyed the game of football until someone kicked the football straight into the next door neighbour's garden.

"Oh dear!" said PC Luca. "Because I'm a policeman, I suppose I'd better go next door and explain what has happened. Will you come with me, Joe?" he asked.

"Of course I will," said Joe.

When the two friends knocked on the door of the neighbour, a nasty witch opened the door.

UNSIGNED PICTURE

"What do you want?" she asked, in her horrible witch's voice.

"May we please have our ball back?" asked PC Luca, politely.

"Why should I give you back your ball?" said the Wicked Witch.

"All my friends have come for a barbeque and want to play football," said Joe.

"And why didn't you invite me then?" asked the witch. "Because you didn't ask me to come to your barbeque, I'm not going to let you have your ball back, so there!"

And so saying, she slammed the door in their faces.

"What a horrid witch!" said PC Luca.

"I suppose we'll have to play something else," said Joe sadly. The two friends went back to Joe's garden and told the others what had happened.

"Never mind," said Fred the Dragon. "We can always play something else."

Everybody played different games; some played snakes and ladders and some played snap and everyone enjoyed themselves. When it was time for everyone to go home, they thanked Joe for a lovely afternoon. Joe said goodbye to everyone and closed the front door.

"I'd better go into the garden and clear up," he thought.

As he was clearing up, Joe thought he heard someone calling his name.

Joe stood very still and listened hard. Yes, there it was again: Someone was calling his name, and it seemed to be coming from next door. Joe looked over the fence and there was the football, tied up and looking very sad.

"Don't you worry, Football, I'll get you out of there," said Joe.

"How will you do it?" asked Football.

"Leave it to me," said Joe, and he went up to his bedroom and found his magic wand in his toy box. Very quietly, he tip-toed out into the garden again and climbed over the fence into the Wicked Witch's garden.

Joe untied Football and was about to climb back over the fence when Football said, "I'm afraid I can't climb your fence: You see, being a football and being rather round, I can't climb.

"I see," said Joe. "Let me put on my thinking cap."

Joe thought and thought and then had a very good idea. He waved his magic wand at Football and said, "Abracadabra."

All of a sudden, Football sprouted legs.

"Look at me!" he said. "Now I can walk just like you, Joe."

"We'd better hurry," said Joe. "We can walk round to the front, but if we don't walk quickly, the Wicked Witch will capture us."

Football followed Joe, but just before they could reach Joe's house, the Wicked Witch appeared.

"What have we here?" she asked. "Who is stealing my football?"

"I'm not your football," said Football. "I belong to Joe."

"Oh you do, do you?" said the Wicked Witch.

"Yes he does," said Joe.

"We'll see about that," said the witch and she waved her magic wand.

"All of a sudden, Joe and Football found themselves locked in a very high tower."

"How are we going to get out of this?" Joe thought.

He looked over at Football, and had an idea.

"If I call for the witch to come, can you use your new legs and run out behind her and escape down the stairs?" He asked. "Then find Fred the Dragon, and ask him to rescue me."

"I'll try," said Football.

So Joe called for the Wicked Witch.

"What do you want?" she asked, through the door.

"We're hungry and thirsty," said Joe. "Can you let us have some food and drink please?"

"Oh, all right," she said, and she went to her kitchen to get some food.

"Now stand behind the door, and when she comes in, you run out on your new legs!" said Joe.

Just then, they heard the key turn in the lock and the door opened with a creak. Quick as a flash, Football ran out and raced down the stairs. The Wicked Witch couldn't catch him, but just in time she remembered to lock the door so Joe couldn't get out.

"You'll have to stay there all night," said the Wicked Witch, and she left. Joe sat on the bed in the tower and waited.

He hadn't waited very long, when he heard the flapping of wings.

"Joe," a voice called him from the window, and when Joe looked out, there was Fred the Dragon. "Quickly, climb on my back before the witch comes," he said.

Joe climbed out of the window onto Fred's back, and soon the two friends were flying towards Joe's home. The walking football was waiting for them.

"That is a very brave football," said Fred. "He walked all the way to Dragonland to tell me all about the Wicked Witch and how she had captured you in the tower and that is why I am here.

"Well done," said Joe to Football, "I knew you could do it. Now we must teach that Wicked Witch a lesson."

Joe picked up his magic wand and went to the house next door. He knocked on the door, and just as the Wicked Witch answered the door, Joe shouted, "Abracadabra!" all at once the Wicked Witch was turned into a football.

"I would like to be the first person to kick her," said Football.

Football took a big run on his new legs and kicked the Wicked Witch football so hard that she disappeared.

"I've never seen a walking football before," said Fred the Dragon.

"And I've never seen a kicking football," said Joe, laughing.

"Can you change me back now please?" asked Football, "I would like to play proper football with you from now on."

MARION PRUD'HON aged 8

163

Joe waved his magic wand once again, and the football's legs disappeared.

"You can kick me now!" said Football, and Joe kicked him so hard, Football went straight into the goal.

"Yippee!" shouted Football. "That's what I really enjoy!"

Everyone agreed that to play football, you really shouldn't have a football that has legs. Fred and Joe played football all afternoon, until it was time to go home.

Joe took Football, and put him in the toy box.

"I'm pleased to see you looking happier," said Joe.

"Thank you, Joe," said Football, "all I ever really wanted was to play with you."

And they all lived happily ever after.

JOE AND THE DUCK

Once upon a time, in a land far, far away, lived a little boy called Joe. Joe lived with his Mummy and Daddy in a house in the country.

One day, Joe was walking to the village, when he heard someone crying, and when Joe turned the corner there was a duckling in the middle of the road with tears in his eyes.

"Whatever is the matter?" asked Joe.

"I've lost my Mummy and Daddy," said the duckling.

"When did you last see them?" asked Joe.

"At breakfast, this morning," said the duckling.

Joe bent down and held the duckling's little wing in his hand.

"Let's see if we can find them, shall we?"

Joe and the duckling started to walk towards the village. They hadn't gone very far when they heard a police car siren, and PC Luca came racing round the corner in his police car. When PC Luca saw his best friend, Joe, he screeched to a halt.

"Hello, Joe," he said, "who's that with you?"

But before Joe could say anything, the duckling said, "I've lost my Mummy and Daddy."

"You'd better get into my police car," said PC Luca, "and we'll go and look for them right away."

They hadn't gone very far when they saw Mr and Mrs Duck. As PC Luca stopped the car, Mrs Duck cried out, "Oh, PC Luca, have you seen my little duckling? We lost him about an hour ago."

"Do you mean this little fellow?" smiled PC Luca.

Mr and Mrs Duck quacked with joy when they saw their little duckling. "Thank you, thank you!" they said.

"Don't thank me, thank Joe. It was Joe who found your duckling."

"Oh, thank you Joe," they both said.

"The problem is that we were supposed to go on holiday, but we didn't have any money and our duckling was so disappointed we were not going, he must have wandered off. Thank you, once again." And taking the little duckling's wing, they waddled up to the village duck pond and were soon swimming about, and having a wonderful time.

"Well done, Joe," said PC Luca. "You've made the ducks very happy. Where do you want to go now?"

"I'd like to see Fred the Dragon," said Joe.

"Well, let me give you a lift to the station and you can take the train to Dragonland from there," said PC Luca.

Off went the two friends and they soon arrived at the station. Joe got out and waved goodbye to PC Luca, who drove off in his nice shiny police car. Joe went into the station to buy a ticket, but the ticket office was closed, so Joe went in search of Mr Smith the Station Master. At Mr Smith's cottage he knocked at the door. Mr Smith opened the door and was pleased to see Joe.

"Oh, Mr Smith," said Joe, "I wanted to go to Dragonland, but the ticket office was closed and I couldn't buy a ticket."

"That's because we can't run any trains today," said Mr Smith.

"Why ever not?" asked Joe.

"The whole of the railway is flooded," said Mr Smith. "You see, when the new lake was built last year, they put in a special gate to hold all the water back when it rained hard. Unfortunately, the gate swung open and all the water is pouring onto the railway lines and we can't run the trains." Then Mr Smith turned to Joe and said, "Joe, can you put on your thinking cap and see if you can come up with an answer?"

MIA WELSH aged 7

Joe thought and thought, and an idea slowly came to him. "Yes," he said, "I think I know a way to help you. Give me a while and I will be back."

Joe waved goodbye to Mr Smith and headed for the village. He went straight to the duck pond and spoke with Mr Duck. Mr Duck was delighted to see Joe, especially as he had found his little duckling. When Joe explained what he wanted, Mr Duck was even more delighted to be of help to him. Joe walked back to Mr Smith's cottage and told Mr Smith not to worry. Soon, all his troubles would be at an end. Mr Smith could hardly believe his ears.

"You mean, you have had an idea how to stop the railway from flooding?" He asked Joe.

"Leave it to me," said Joe.

In the meantime, Joe decided that, because the railway wasn't working, he may as well go home. Joe had an early night and the next day, after he had had breakfast and got dressed, he walked to the station. When he got there, he was pleased to see that the ticket office was open, and lots and lots of people were buying tickets. When Mr Smith saw him, he came over to Joe.

"How can I ever thank you, Joe? The railway is open and all the water has disappeared. However did you manage it?"

"I asked my friend, Mr Duck to bring all his friends to the new gate on the lake, and try and close it. As soon as it was closed, all the water stopped pouring through and the railway dried out."

"Just for that, you shall have a special ticket to Dragonland free of charge."

"Thank you," said Joe, "but instead of giving me a ticket, can you give it to Mr Duck and his family, so they can go on holiday."

Mr Smith put his hand on his chin and thought. "I'm not sure about that," he said. "Leave it with me and I'll see what I can do. In the meantime, take your ticket to Dragonland and give my regards to Fred and his family."

P.C. Luca

BELINDA CARINI-NUN aged 7

Joe took the ticket and got on the train to Dragonland. He and Fred had a wonderful day playing with all of Fred's toys, and when it was time to go home, Mrs Dragon asked Joe if he could come back again soon.

"Of course I can," said Joe.

On the journey home, Joe looked out of the train's window and was pleased to see that people were sailing boats and rowing around on the new lake. "Better than being flooded," he thought. "A lake is where the water belongs, not all over the railway."

Joe walked back to the village from the station and when he got to the village duck pond, he was disappointed that Mr and Mrs Duck and their family were nowhere to be seen.

"That's funny," he thought, and because they were not there, Joe decided to walk home. He hadn't gone very far, when he met Mrs Pig.

"Have you seen the Duck family?" asked Joe.

"No, they seem to have disappeared," said Mrs Pig.

The next person Joe met was Mr Lavender, the farmer. "Have you seen the duck family?" Joe asked him.

"Not for ages," said Farmer Lavender.

Joe was now getting a bit worried. "I think I will go and ask PC Luca to help find them," he thought. When he found PC Luca, he told him that Mr and Mrs Duck and their family were nowhere to be found.

"I've asked Mrs Pig, and she thinks that they may have disappeared. I asked Farmer Lavender, and he said that he hadn't seen them for ages. I don't know where they can be."

"Now, don't you worry," said PC Luca. "Why don't you go home, and tomorrow we can go to Dragonland together."

"But why would I want to go to Dragonland, when we have to find Mr and Mrs Duck and her family?" asked Joe. But PC Luca just smiled and waved goodbye, as he drove off in his police car.

ELLA BAILEY aged 9

"That's very strange behaviour," Joe said to himself, and shrugged. "Oh well, I suppose if no one can help find the Duck family, I'd better go home," he said.

The next day Joe was having breakfast with his Mummy and Daddy, when there was a knock at the front door. When Joe opened the door, there was PC Luca.

"Are you ready yet, Joe?" He asked.

"I'm just having breakfast," Joe said.

"As soon as you are ready, we can go to Dragonland," said PC Luca.

Joe finished breakfast and said goodbye to Mummy and Daddy, and soon he and PC Luca were driving to the station to go to Dragonland. But when they got to the station, the ticket office was closed again.

"Oh dear," said Joe, "it looks like another day of trouble."

"Come with me," said PC Luca.

The two friends walked to platform number one and there was Mr Smith waiting with Tanky the train.

"But I didn't think anyone was here," said Joe, "because the ticket office was closed."

"It's closed because today is a very special day," said Mr Smith. "Because you were so clever, you saved the railway, and here is another special ticket to Dragonland to say thank you."

So saying, Mr Smith handed a special ticket to Joe. "Now, if you climb aboard Tanky, we will be off to Dragonland immediately."

Off they all went and soon they were whizzing through the countryside.

"There's the new lake, which thanks to you and Mr Duck and his friends, is full with the water that had flooded the railway," said Mr Smith. They rounded a bend and there was Dragonland station.

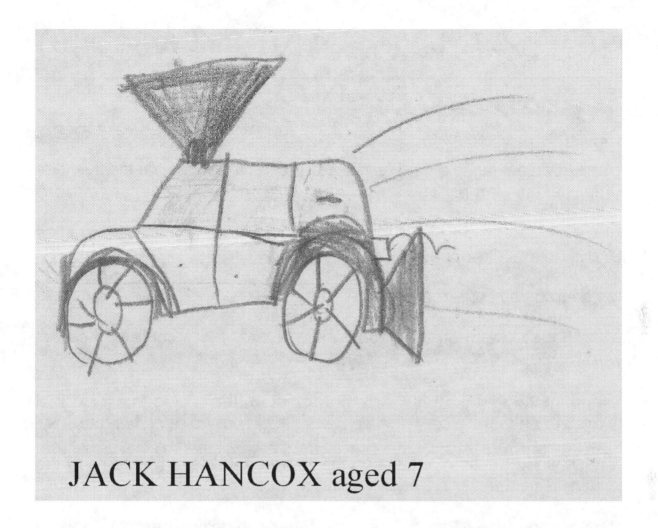

JACK HANCOX aged 7

On the station were lots of people, including Fred the Dragon. As Joe got off the train, he was delighted to see Mr and Mrs Duck and their family. PC Luca laughed and explained that they had been here all week enjoying the holiday that they could not afford, all paid for by the railway company to say thank you to them for all their help.

"And this is for you from the railway company. Thanks once again, Joe," said Mr Smith, and gave Joe a huge chocolate cake.

Joe was very happy. After all, it is always nice to cheer people up and help them.

And they all lived happily ever after.

JOE AND GRANDMA AND GRANDPA

Once upon a time, in a land far, far away, lived a little boy called Joe. Joe lived with his Mummy and Daddy in a house in the country.

One day, Joe asked his Mummy and Daddy if he could go to visit his Grandma and Grandpa.

"Of course you can," they said.

"Why not call them on the phone and ask if they can come and collect you?" said Mummy.

"Good idea," said Joe, and he went to phone them. Joe arranged that Grandma and Grandpa would come and pick him up at eleven o'clock.

"That's when the little hand is on the eleven and the big hand is on the twelve," said Joe.

"That's very clever," said Grandma. "That's exactly when we shall be there."

At exactly eleven o'clock, Grandma and Grandpa arrived, and off they went.

"Shall we go and get an ice cream?" they asked.

"Yes please," said Joe. "May I have a chocolate one please?"

"Of course you can," they said.

But when they got to the ice cream shop, the man who sold the ice cream was very upset.

"What's wrong?" asked Joe.

OLIVIA KING aged 9

"We've run out of ice cream," said the man. "Yesterday was so hot that all the boys and girls had at least three ice creams each, and now we haven't got any left, and the weather is getting hot again and I need some more ice cream for all the boys and girls who have not had their ice creams yet."

"What are you going to do?" asked Grandma.

"If you could go to where they make the ice cream and bring me some back, I would be very grateful," said the man.

That's all Joe needed to hear. "Do you know where the ice cream comes from, Grandma and Grandpa?" he asked.

"It comes from Iceberg Ices, near Dragonland," Grandpa said.

"Then let's go there now and get some right away," said Joe.

They all got into Grandma and Grandpa's car and drove to Iceberg Ices.

When they went inside, the man who makes the ice cream was very upset.

"What's wrong?" asked Joe.

"Yesterday was so hot," said the man, "that all the boys and girls ate up all the ice cream I was making, and now we haven't any left to send to the shops."

"How long will it be before you can make some more?" asked Joe.

"I don't think that any ice cream will be ready until next Tuesday," said the man. "Can you put on your thinking cap please, Joe?" He asked, "and see if you can find a way out of the problem?"

Joe thought and thought, and then had a brilliant idea.

"Grandma and Grandpa, can you drive me to Dragonland so that we can find my friend, Fred the Dragon?"

"Of course we can," they said.

ADAM MARKS aged 8

"Now don't you worry," said Joe to the ice cream man. "I'll be back very soon with my Grandma and Grandpa with lots and lots of lovely things so you can make some more ice cream."

"Oh, thank you Joe," said the man.

Joe and Grandma and Grandpa drove off to dragon land.

"Fred the Dragon lives in the second house in the street, Grandpa," said Joe.

When Grandpa stopped at the first house by mistake, Joe said, "Silly old Grandpa; not the first house, the second one!"

"Oops! Sorry Joe!" said Grandpa.

They soon stopped at Fred's house and got out. Fred was playing in the front garden, and was delighted to see Joe, Grandma and Grandpa.

"I haven't got time to play today," said Joe. "I have to ask you to do something very special for me."   And Joe whispered in his friend's ear.

"Hop on board," said Fred to Joe, Grandma and Grandpa, "and we'll take off right away."

Grandma, Grandpa and Joe climbed onto Fred's back and with a run and a hop and an enormous jump, Fred was soon flying over the roof tops.

"This is fun," said Grandma and Grandpa.

"I've never been up in the sky on a dragon before," said Grandpa.

"Neither have I," said Grandma.

"Sit back and enjoy the ride," said Fred.

"We've got rather a long way to go," said Joe.

Off they flew, and before long Grandma said that she was starting to feel very cold. Soon Grandpa said to Joe, "Don't you feel cold, Joe?"

"You'll see why it's getting so cold very soon," said Joe as they flew on.

"We're nearly there," said Fred.

"There it is," said Joe, and pointed to a huge mountain.

But it wasn't an ordinary mountain: This mountain was made of ice cream and had an enormous red cherry at the top of it.

"Wherever are we?" asked Grandma.

"Why, this is the North Pole!" said Joe.

"And what is that huge mountain?" asked Grandpa.

"That's the Ice Cream Mountain, where all the things to make ice cream come from."

Fred the Dragon landed, and Joe waved to everyone. "Come on everybody, we haven't a moment to lose," and he walked towards the mountain.

"Do you have an appointment?" asked a voice, and they all looked down to see a little man, standing at the foot of the mountain.

The little man was dressed in a rather large ice cream cornet and was wearing a very large chocolate biscuit for a hat.

"An appointment?" asked Joe.

"No one is allowed to climb the ice cream mountain without an appointment," said the little man. "I mean after all, if everyone was allowed to come here, we wouldn't have any ice cream ingredients left at all, now would we?"

"I suppose not," said Fred, "but Joe hasn't come for an ice cream for himself, he's come to make sure that Iceberg Ices can have the things to make the ice cream for their ice cream shop, so that all the boys and girls can have some ice cream."

"Well that's different," said the little man. "I always like to hear that someone is being kind. Follow me everyone!" and the little man walked up a steep path made of strawberry snowflakes and chocolate pebbles.

They hadn't gone very far when the little man asked Grandpa to pick up a bucket, and he filled it with lots of the chocolate pebbles. The little man then gave Joe another bucket, and asked him to put the stones made of lemon into his bucket.

"What shall we carry?" asked Fred, pointing at himself and Grandma.

"Carry these please," said the little man, and gave them an armful of wafers each.

"There, that should be enough to be getting on with," said the little man.

Joe thanked him for all his help, soon Grandma, Grandpa and Joe were on Fred's back flying over the ice fields of the North Pole, on their way home.

"I must say that it is much nicer to be going home," said Grandma. "I'm feeling warmer already."

Soon, Fred landed right next to Iceberg Ices. When the man saw what Joe and everyone had brought him, he was very excited.

"Why, you're so clever, Joe," he said. "Now I can make enough chocolate and lemon ice cream for all the boys and girls; the only problem is, will you be able to deliver the ice cream before it all melts?"

"Don't worry about that," said Joe. "After all, Fred is here, and he can carry some of the ice cream on his back, and Grandma and Grandpa can put the rest in their car."

"Great idea," said the man, and went off to make the ice cream.

After a while the man came out of Iceberg Ices with lots and lots of ice cream.

"Why don't you take the first load to the ice cream shop, on Fred's back?" asked Grandpa. "Grandma and I will bring the rest in our car."

"You're right, Grandpa. I'd better hurry because it's getting very hot again, and all the boys and girls will be expecting their ice creams," said Joe.

Joe and Fred said goodbye, and were soon on their way to the ice cream shop. When they arrived, the ice cream man was very excited to see so much ice cream. Outside the shop was a long queue of boys and girls, and they all cheered Joe and Fred when they saw what they had brought.

The ice cream man started to sell the ice cream and soon realised that he was running out of ice cream again.

"Don't worry," said Joe. "There's more on the way."

Just then they heard a police siren and there, coming down the village street was Grandma and Grandpa driving in their car, behind PC Luca's shiny police car.

HANNAH ROSE BERGER aged 7

BY HANNAH ROSE BERGER.

"I saw them out in the country and when they told me they had to get here fast, I just had to help," said PC Luca.

"Thank you, PC Luca. They've certainly arrived just in time," said Joe.

At last, all the boys and girls had been given enough ice cream.

"And now it's your turn," said the ice cream man. "I can't thank you all enough. Joe, you really saved the day." The ice cream man gave Joe, Grandma, Grandpa and Fred so much ice cream they had to have it for breakfast, lunch and supper for two weeks before it had all gone.

And they all lived happily ever after.

AYDAN DOYLE aged 10

cupboard

JOE AND THE CUPBOARD

Once upon a time, in a land far, far away, lived a little boy called Joe. Joe lived with his Mummy and Daddy in a house in the country.

One day, Joe's Mummy and Daddy asked him if he could tidy up his toy cupboard. "It's not because it is in a mess," said Mummy, "I just need you to go through the toys and separate the toys you want to keep from those we can give away."

Off Joe went and opened his toy cupboard. "Good morning, Joe," said the cupboard.

"Good morning," said Joe, rather startled. "I didn't know you could speak."

"Well, only on clean-up days," said the cupboard. "You see, I think it good to speak to the boys and girls, to help them when they want to clean me up."

"I don't know where to start," said Joe.

"Exactly! So why not take all your toys and line them all up and then you can see which are the ones you don't play with any more, and choose those toys you like to play with all the time?"

"Good idea, Mr Cupboard," said Joe.

Joe picked up a box and looked at a label on it: It said Joe's first game.

"Do you recognise that game?" asked the cupboard.

"Of course," said Joe. "This is my first game that I had, when I was a baby."

"So you probably don't ever play with that anymore," said cupboard. "Put that on the pile of toys not wanted," he said.

As Joe put it on the unwanted pile, the box started to cry. "Waagh, waagh!" it went, just like a baby crying.

"That's the trouble with baby games," said cupboard. "They cry when they are put down. Now, what's the next toy to be looked at?"

Joe looked over at the garage in the corner. "I won't be putting that away," he said. "I like playing with the garage."

"Then put it on a separate pile, for all the toys you want to keep," said cupboard.

As Joe put it on the pile of toys to be played with, the garage said, "Broom, broom!"

Joe smiled and so he went on until he had, with the help of cupboard, made two piles of toys: The ones he wanted to play with, and those he would give away to other children.

"Are you going to play with anything right now?" asked the cupboard.

"I think I'll play with my garage," said Joe, and he took the garage out of the cupboard. Joe had a lovely morning, playing with the garage until he heard Mummy calling to him from the kitchen.

"Lunch is ready!" she called.

"I'm coming!" said Joe, and put the garage back in the cupboard.

"I expect it will be a while until we speak again," said cupboard. "After all, it isn't every day you clean me up, is it?"

"Would you like to speak to me more then?" asked Joe.

"That would be very nice," said the cupboard. "Far better than waiting here for cleanup day."

"Then as soon as I have had my lunch, I'll come and have a nice chat with you," said Joe, and he zoomed off downstairs for his lunch.

"Who were you talking to in your bedroom, Joe?" asked Mummy.

"I was talking to my toy cupboard," said Joe.

"Your toy cupboard?" said Daddy. "I've never heard of anyone talking to a toy cupboard before."

Joe smiled, but didn't say anything else until he had finished his lunch.

"That was a very nice lunch, Mummy, thank you. May I leave the table now?" he asked.

"Of course you may," said Mummy, and Joe disappeared upstairs and into his bedroom.

"I missed you," said the cupboard.

"My Daddy thinks talking to a cupboard is very strange." said Joe.

"Well there are lots of cupboards who can't talk, and look at the mess they are in," said the cupboard. "Now, I'm glad we are having a little chat, because I have something very important to ask you."

"What is it you want?" asked Joe.

"I have a cousin living next door, who has a nasty witch for his owner. He never ever has a chat, and the inside of his cupboard is so messy that you can't open it without everything falling out."

"So what can I do?" asked Joe.

"I suppose the best thing would be to make the nasty witch into a nice witch, and then she could clean up her cupboard and make my cousin happy," said the cupboard.

"I'll put on my thinking cap and see what I can do," said Joe.

Joe thought and thought, and had a brilliant idea. He went next door and knocked on the nasty witch's door.

"Who's there?" came a croaky voice.

"It's Joe, from next door," said Joe.

"Well, go away! I don't like little boys!" said the witch.

"Not even if they have come to clean out your cupboard?" asked Joe.

The door opened, and there was the nasty witch.

"Would you really do that?" she asked. "Or are you trying to trick me?"

"Just you see," said Joe and he went into the bedroom and opened the cupboard.

As the cupboard door opened, everything fell out. Now, because Joe had been warned by his own toy cupboard, he had stepped to one side, but the witch who was standing with him did not know that everything would fall out, and all the things in the cupboard landed on top of her, covering her so completely that she was nowhere to be seen.

"That's better," said a voice.

"Who said that?" asked Joe.

"It's me, the witch's cupboard," said a voice.

"Your cousin next door told me all about you," said Joe.

"What he probably didn't tell you," said the witch's cupboard, "is that because I am a witch's cupboard, I can grant you three wishes for being so helpful, Joe. What is your first wish?"

Joe thought and thought.

"My first wish is to have a lovely party for all of my friends, with lots and lots of chocolate cake and milk and fruit juice and loads of lovely toys."

"When would you like the party?" asked the cupboard.

"At the weekend please," said Joe.

"Your wish is granted," said the cupboard. "What is your second wish Joe?"

"I want the nasty witch to be a nice witch, and keep her cupboard tidy," said Joe.

"Your second wish is granted," said the cupboard.

There was a big bang and a flash, and all the things that had fallen out flew back into the witch's cupboard all very neatly and tidily. Some things piled on shelves and other things properly put in a very tidy order. How nice everything looked when it was done.

"Would you like to have an ice cream?" said a voice. When Joe turned round there was a beautiful lady holding an enormous ice cream.

"Who are you?" asked Joe.

"Why, I was once a nasty witch, and because of you and your wish, you have made me into a nice witch, and I look forward to always having an ice cream ready for you, whenever you want it," she said.

Joe was delighted, especially when he found that there were loads of strawberries in the ice cream. When he finished his ice cream, the witch took him downstairs and gave him a new toy train to take home.

"Will you come to my party at the weekend?" Joe asked.

"I certainly will," said the witch.

When Joe got home, he immediately went to his cupboard and told him all about the nasty witch and how his cousin's cupboard was now tidy. But the cupboard didn't answer.

"Can't you talk anymore?" Joe asked, but there was silence.

When Joe told his Mummy and Daddy all about the two cupboards, they laughed. "You must have been dreaming," they said, and Joe had to agree that maybe he had imagined the whole thing. But what he did do was ask his Mummy and Daddy if they could have a party at the weekend, and invite all his friends, and especially the witch from next door.

Joe was very pleased when they agreed.

The weekend arrived, and all Joe's friends came to his party.

"Shall we eat in the garden?" asked Mummy, and everyone thought it a great idea.

Fred the Dragon, PC Luca and Annabelle sat at a long table in the garden. The nice witch from next door sat down, and Mummy and Daddy both said that they didn't remember the witch being so beautiful. Joe just smiled because he knew why she looked so good. Mummy and Daddy brought out delicious sandwiches and the biggest chocolate cake.

Just then, it started to rain.

"Oh no!" everyone shouted. "We'll all get wet now."

"I don't think so," said Joe, and closed his eyes.

"I wish it was a nice sunny day," he said.

All at once, the sun came out.

"How did you do that?" everyone asked Joe, but Joe just smiled, because he remembered he still had that one last wish left.

And they all lived happily ever after.

ZARA BRACEDAY aged 7

JOE AND THE PIRATES

Once upon a time, in a land far, far away, lived a little boy called Joe. Joe lived with his Mummy and Daddy in a house in the country.

One day, Joe was playing in the garden all by himself when he heard a noise.

Joe looked all around but couldn't see anyone. "Is anybody there?" He asked.

"It's me," said a voice, and a pirate came from where he had been hiding behind some bushes. The pirate had a long red beard and was dressed just like a pirate should be, with a huge sword tucked into his belt.

"Hello," said Joe, "I don't believe we have met."

"That would be mainly because I've never been here before. How do you do? My name is Red Bearded Sid, and I come from a ship that is floating in the river nearby, and I am looking for someone called Joe.

"That's me! I'm Joe!"

"Shiver me timbers, me hearty. Fancy meeting you so quickly; I was getting worried that I might not get to see you."

"Now that you have found me," said Joe, "how may I help you?"

"It's my ship; we have a problem: The main mast, the big pole that holds up the sail, needs to be replaced. The problem is that because we are

pirates we can't get anyone to help us and when we spoke to PC Luca, he said that you were the only person he could think of, who could tell us where to get help."

"Can I come to see your ship?" Said Joe.

"Of course you can, me hearty. Ha-harr!"

JOSEPH REISSNER aged 8

"Why do you speak like that?" asked Joe.

"All pirates speak like that," said Red Bearded Sid. "It's what makes us pirates and different from say, a milkman or a farmer."

"I see," said Joe. "Shall we go to your ship now?"

"Follow me, Joe, but because we are pirates, I have to blindfold you so that you can't tell anyone where we are hiding."

"But isn't that a bit silly? After all, I'm going to have to see where the ship is so that I can bring you a new mast," said Joe."

PC Luca told me you were clever! Yes, you're right Joe, I shall trust you not to give away our secret hiding place. Follow me, me hearty and I'll take you to the ship," said Red Bearded Sid.

Off they went through the bushes, and soon they came to a path that ran alongside a river. They turned a corner, and there was a magnificent pirate ship. It had huge guns called canons, sticking out the side. Leading from the ship was a long plank of wood.

"What's that plank of wood for?" asked Joe.

"That's for making naughty people walk the plank," said Red Bearded Sid.

"And what happens to them?" asked Joe.

"Why, they drop off the end into the water," said Red Bearded Sid.

"That's not very nice," said Joe.

"Oh we haven't had anyone walk the plank for ages, it's not politically correct," said Red Bearded Sid.

"What does that mean?" asked Joe.

"I heard it somewhere," said Red Bearded Sid.

They walked on board the ship where Joe found lots of other pirates who were all very pleased to see him.

JOSHUA BURNS aged 8

"We heard you can help us, Joe," they all said.

"Would you like to show me what the problem is Red Bearded Sid?" said Joe.

"Well, you can see for yourself, Joe. The top part of the mast is broken. You see, we were sailing through a storm and a big wave snapped the top right off, and that's why we need a new one. PC Luca told us that you have a very good thinking cap and can find the answer to any problem."

So Joe put on his thinking cap. Where was he to find a new mast for the pirate ship? It was quite a problem.

"While you are thinking," said Red Bearded Sid, "would you like to have a pirate supper with us?"

"Oh, thank you. I would, yes please," said Joe.

"Then follow me," said Red Bearded Sid. "And you had better have a sword just in case of trouble."

LIOR SHARON aged 9

Red Bearded Sid gave Joe an enormous sword and then all the pirates marched off the ship holding their swords as well. They hadn't gone very far when they saw another pirate ship.

"Come on Joe," shouted Red Bearded Sid, "our supper has been stolen by the other pirates and we have to get it back."

All the pirates and Joe ran onto the other ship waving their swords above their heads, the other pirates were so scared when they saw Joe with his sword, that they all ran away.

"Thank you, Joe," said Red Bearded Sid, we don't normally frighten anyone, but when they saw you, the other pirates must have heard that you were a good fighter and ran away."

"Now we can have our supper," shouted all the pirates.

All the pirates and Joe sat down to pirate roast chicken, with pirate potatoes and pirate broccoli. When they had finished eating, all the pirates ran to the side of the ship.

"What are they doing?" asked Joe.

"They're all washing their plates in the river," said Red bearded Sid.

"That's a good idea," said Joe, and he washed his plate as well.

"Have you thought of a way to get a new mast for our ship yet?" asked Red Bearded Sid.

"I think I have," said Joe, "but because you are all pirates, we may have a bit of trouble getting it. I think you should come along with me to the police station first."

So along to the police station went all the pirates, led by Red Bearded Sid. When they got there Joe asked them all to wait outside while he went into the police station to see PC Luca.

"Hello Joe," said PC Luca. "Has Red Bearded Sid the pirate found you yet?"

MELODY WHITE aged 9

OLIVIA ROBINSON aged 9

"That's why I'm here," said Joe. "I've thought of a way to get a new mast for the pirate ship, but all the pirates have to promise not to do any pirating near my house, so I want you to get them to make a promise, because you are a policeman," said Joe.

PC Luca and Joe went outside the police station.

PC Luca asked all the pirates to promise not to do any pirating near Joe's house, and they all agreed.

"Now will you tell us where we can get a new mast?" asked Red Bearded Sid.

"Come with me," said Joe.

Joe took all the pirates to his garden and pointed to a tree. "You see that tree; when I feel tired I often have a sleep under it, but because you have all promised to be good pirates, I'm going to let you have it for your new mast," said Joe. "But you have to promise to plant two young trees in its place so they can grow to be big enough to sleep under."

197

Red Bearded Sid was delighted. He asked some of his pirates to chop down the old tree and plant two new ones.

The next day Joe had a phone call. "Can you come down to the river now, Joe?" asked Red Bearded Sid.

"Yes I can," said Joe, and off he went.

When he got to the river, there was the pirate ship, complete with its new mast. A big sail was set and the ship was floating out to sea. All the pirates were waving and shouting 'thank you' to Joe. At the back of the ship was a huge flag called the Jolly Roger, a special pirate flag.

"Put your fingers in your ears, Joe," shouted Red Bearded Sid, and Joe did as he was told, just as all the guns went bang.

"That was our pirate way of thanking you," said Red Bearded Sid, and waved a final goodbye to Joe, and all the pirates cheered together.

And they all lived happily ever after.

MOLLIE CATLIN aged 10

JOE AND THE HOUSE BADGE

Once upon a time, in a land far, far away, lived a little boy called Joe. Joe lived with his Mummy and Daddy in a house in the country.

One day, Joe was getting ready for school. He got dressed and had his breakfast and then he cleaned his teeth, and waited by the front door for Mummy to take him to school in her car.

Daddy was going away for his work and would not be back for two days. As Joe waited for Mummy, he waved goodbye to his Daddy, who drove away in his car.

Today Joe was especially excited, because today was the day that the house badge was going to be given to the most well behaved boy in the class. Joe had remembered to shake hands with his teachers every day. Of course he had said please and thank you, but then he always did, and had always held the door open when people needed to come and go in his classroom.

He hoped his teacher would remember him when she decided who was to have the house badge.

"Hurry up Mummy," said Joe. "I'm ready for school."

"Coming," Mummy called, as she reached the bottom of the stairs, but just as she ran towards him, she tripped on the carpet and hurt her ankle.

"Are you all right, Mummy?" asked Joe.

Mummy sat on the bottom step of the stairs and held her ankle.

"I think I've twisted my ankle, Joe," she said. "Oh dear, now you'll be late for school. What are we to do?"

"I know just the person to help," Joe said.

Joe went to the telephone.

"Is that you, PC Luca?" Mummy heard him ask. "Can you come to my house right away please? Mummy has hurt her ankle and Daddy has gone away, and I need someone to take her to the doctor."

Joe put down the phone and went back to Mummy.

"Don't worry, Mummy," he said, "PC Luca is on his way to take you to the doctor."

Just then, they heard PC Luca's siren, and a knock on the door told them that he had arrived.

Very carefully, Joe and PC Luca helped Mummy into the shiny police car, and off they went. When they got to the doctor, he bandaged Mummy's ankle and said that she must have lots of rest, until the ankle was better.

"At least a day in bed will put it right," he said.

By the time PC Luca and Joe took Mummy home, Joe had completely forgotten about school and the house badge. PC Luca and Joe helped Mummy up to bed, and then PC Luca went off to the kitchen to make a nice cup of tea.

"Is there anything that you need?" asked Joe.

"I think that if I am to be in bed, it would be very nice to have a book from the library to read," she said.

Just then, PC Luca came in holding a tray with tea and biscuits.

"Why don't I give you a lift to the library in my police car, Joe," he said.

So, making sure that Mummy was comfortable, Joe and PC Luca drove off to the library. PC Luca dropped Joe off and waved goodbye, as Joe shouted his thanks to the very helpful policeman.

Then, Joe entered the library to get Mummy a book. Because it was for a grown up, he asked Miss Binder the librarian what she could recommend. Miss Binder climbed some steps and took a book from quite high up.

"I'm sure she will like this one," she said.

"Joe thanked her, and as he left the library, who should be walking along the street but his friend Annabelle.

"Why, Joe, shouldn't you be in school?" she asked.

"Goodness me," said Joe. "School! I forgot all about school! I must call them right away! Thank you, Annabelle. It's a good thing we met, or I would have forgotten completely."

Joe went back into the library and asked Miss Binder if he might use her telephone to call his teacher.

"Of course you can, Joe," she said.

But when Joe called, there was no answer.

"Oh dear," he thought, "they're all at the house badge ceremony and cannot hear the phone ringing. I'd better take the book back to Mummy and then go to school to let them know what I've been doing."

He thanked Miss Binder and was soon on his way home. He hadn't gone very far when he heard someone crying for help.

"Help, help," went the voice.

"Where are you?" asked Joe.

"Down here," said the voice, and Joe looked down to see that at the side of the road was a ditch and a little black cat had fallen into the muddy water and had got stuck.

"I'll have you out of there as quickly as I can," said Joe, putting the library book down in a dry safe place. Joe rolled up his sleeves and knelt down at the side of the ditch and grabbed hold of the little black cat. He pulled very hard, and with a loud squelching noise he managed to pull the cat free of the mud at the bottom of the ditch.

"Oh, thank you so much," said the cat. "What is your name, so I can thank you properly?"

"My name is Joe," said Joe.

"Well, thank you Joe. I was just on my way to my new job, and you have helped me to get there on time. Thank you once again." And with a swish of his tail, the cat disappeared into the woods behind them.

By the time Joe got to his house and looked at the clock, he realised that he was too late for school and would have to wait until the next day before he could explain to his teacher what had stopped him from getting to school.

Mummy was delighted with the book, and Joe told Mummy not to worry, because he was going to make sure that she had a lovely supper and a fine breakfast in the morning.

Joe made his Mummy some yummy scrambled eggs with bread and butter for supper, and then cleaned his teeth ready for bed himself. He went into Mummy to make sure she was alright, before giving her a special good night, and get well kiss.

Joe went to bed and was soon fast asleep.

In the morning, he went to see how his Mummy was and was delighted that she was sitting up, feeling much better.

"Now don't you worry Joe, I'm well enough to drive you to school today."

"Then, while you are getting ready I'm going to make you a lovely breakfast," said Joe, and he did.

Mummy and Joe drove to school. When Joe arrived, he waved goodbye to Mummy and went to his classroom.

When he got there, his teacher was very cross with him.

"Didn't you know that yesterday was a very important day?" She said.

"But I…" and that was all that Joe managed to say, before his teacher said that he must sit on the naughty step until she called him.

All morning, the school children went passed him, but no one was allowed to talk to him.

ROSS McKENDRICK aged 10

When his teacher passed by, he went to say, "but I..." but before he could say anything else, she had disappeared into another classroom.

Joe sat there, feeling very sorry for himself, when he heard a 'meow' behind him. Joe turned to see the little black and white cat.

"Hello Joe, fancy seeing you here, and sitting on the naughty step; whatever has happened?"

Joe told the little black cat all that had happened the day before, and how his Mummy had been hurt, and by the time he returned from the library he had missed school.

"And don't forget you saved me from the ditch," said the little black cat.

"Well, that was nothing," said Joe.

"Now, just you wait here," said the little black cat, and with a swish of his tail he jumped off the steps and into the classroom corridor. He hadn't been gone very long before his teacher came back with the little black cat.

"Oh Joe, I must apologise and say how sorry I am," said his teacher. "I didn't let you tell me about what had happened, and I really should not have made you sit on the naughty step at all. Why don't you go home early in case your Mummy needs anything, and come to school tomorrow," she said.

Joe went home, and when he arrived he was delighted to see that his Daddy's car was outside the house.

Daddy made quite a fuss of him when Mummy told Daddy what a very clever boy Joe had been the day before.

They all sat down to a special dinner and had not been eating for very long when they heard a police siren and the police car stop outside their house.

"That's funny," said Daddy. "I wonder what PC Luca wants at this time of night."

When the doorbell rang, Joe opened the door and there standing outside was PC Luca; but he was not alone: Standing beside him was Joe's teacher and the little black cat.

"Joe because of your outstanding behaviour," said his teacher, "and for saving our new school cat from the ditch, I have come to give you something."

"Please come inside," said Joe's Mummy and Daddy.

As Joe's teacher stepped into the hall she stooped down and placed something on Joe's pullover and when he looked, it was a shiny new house badge.

"That's for being the best in the class," said his teacher, and the cat smiled and meowed in agreement.

"This calls for a celebration said Mummy; why don't we all sit down and finish our lovely dinner together."

And they did.

And they all lived happily ever after.

JOE AND THE PARK KEEPER

Once upon a time in a land far, far away lived a little boy called Joe. Joe lived with his Mummy and Daddy in a house in the country.

One day, Joe was walking in the park. He loved to play on the swings and the slides and he especially liked the roundabout, where you could sit on the special seat and close your eyes as you went round and round.

The park was empty, because his school had finished for the holidays before any of the others and all the boys and girls were still in their classrooms.

Joe decided that he would try the swings first of all. As he sat on, and began to swing backwards and forwards, he began to feel very tired.

"You shouldn't be on the swing, if you are tired," said a voice.

"I shouldn't?" said Joe.

"No you shouldn't; it's dangerous," said the voice.

"And how do you know that?" asked Joe.

"Because you're sitting on me!" said the voice.

Joe could not help laughing.

"I'm sorry if I seemed rude," said Joe. "Would you like me to get off your seat?"

"Oh no, as long as you are awake and not nodding off, I really enjoy having you play on me," said the voice, "and you do seem to be very good at swinging backwards and forwards. The problem is, I am going to be taken away soon and I am very unhappy."

"Taken away?" said Joe, in surprise. "Why are you being taken away?"

"It's all because of the new park keeper, who doesn't like me very much," said the swing.

"But Mrs Green, the Park Keeper is a very nice lady," said Joe.

"Mrs Green is not here," said the swing. "She went on holiday last week, and this nasty man, Mr Black has taken her job."

"You leave it to me, Mr Swing. I'll try to think of something," said Joe, and he jumped off the swing and waved, as he walked across the park on his way home.

He had not gone very far, when he saw a man, walking towards him.

"Hello," said the man, "are you Joe?"

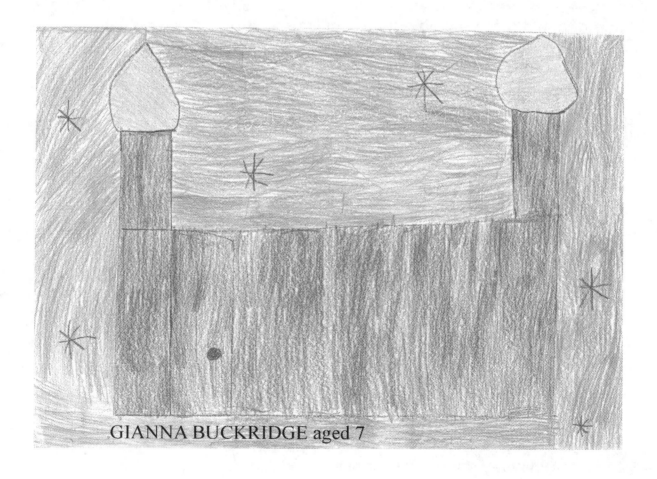

GIANNA BUCKRIDGE aged 7

JOANNA BUCKRIDGE aged 7

"Yes I am," said Joe, puzzled that the man should know his name.

"My name is Mr Black," said the man, and I am the park keeper until Mrs Green comes back from her holiday."

"Mr Swing told me all about you," said Joe. "Is it true that you are going to take him away for scrap?"

Mr Black laughed and laughed. "Of course I'm not," he said.

"But Mr Swing told me, that he was very sad because that was what you are going to do," said Joe.

"Of course I am not. Mrs Green has asked that I have Mr Swing taken to have all his parts made new again. You see, because he stands outside in the rain and snow, Mr Swing's parts have become very rusty. We are going to make him as good as new and give him a lovely coat of new paint, not take him away for scrap."

"I must go and tell him right away," said Joe. "That will cheer him up."

Joe hurried to tell Mr Swing the good news, but when he arrived at the playground at the corner of the park, where all the play things were, there was no sign of Mr Swing. "That's funny," he thought, "I wonder where he could have got to."

Joe looked everywhere in the park for Mr Swing. He looked in the bicycle shed and he was not there. He looked in the big barn where the tractors were kept, but he was not there.

Finally, feeling very tired, he sat down on a park bench.

"I wonder where he could have got to." said Joe, out loud.

"Who are you looking for?" asked a voice.

Joe looked down, and saw a very pretty little Fairy looking at him.

"I'm looking for Mr Swing; he has disappeared. He thinks he is going to be taken away for scrap and it is not true. The park keeper is going to repair him and give him a lovely new coat of paint. I wanted to tell him, and make him happy. Have you any idea where he could have got to?" Joe asked.

"I don't know where he might be," said the Fairy, "but I think I know someone who can help. The trouble is, you are too big to come with me. Would you mind if I cast a spell and made you smaller?"

"Of course you can," said Joe.

"Then Abracadabra," said the Fairy, and Joe suddenly became as small as the little Fairy. "Don't worry, Joe," she said, "as soon as we are finished, I'll change you back to your real size. Now come with me."

Off they went, with the Fairy in the lead.

"Where are we going?" asked Joe.

"We are going to see the Queen of all the fairies, who knows about everything that happens in the park," she said.

As they turned a corner, there in front of them was a palace. Normally, most people would have walked passed it, because it was really rather small, but because Joe was now as small as the little Fairy, it seemed quite big to him.

The Fairy took Joe's hand, and as her hand touched his, they started to fly through the air into the Queen's palace.

The Queen was sitting in the kitchen, having a cup of coffee.

"Hello, Shrubby," she said to the Fairy, "who is that with you?"

"This is Joe, Your Majesty, and he is looking for Mr Swing."

"Mr Swing is under my protection," said the Queen. "A nasty man called Mr Black is going to take him away for scrap, and I cannot allow that to happen."

That is not true, Your Majesty," said Joe, "Mr Swing thinks he is going to be taken for scrap, but really he is going to be given lovely shiny new parts, and painted with bright paint, ready for all the boys and girls to play with him,"

JOSEPH BAKER aged 7

"Is that true?" asked the Queen.

"Yes, it is," said the Fairy and Joe, together.

"Then come with me," said the queen.

Joe held onto the Fairy's hand as the Queen led the way, as they flew to the other side of the park, where the playground was.

When they landed, the queen waved her magic wand at Joe, and he became his real size.

"There is Mr Swing," said the Queen.

"But I cannot see him," said Joe.

"Abracadabra," said the Queen, and lo and behold, Mr Swing suddenly appeared. "I had made him invisible, and he was here all the time," said the Queen.

RAYONA MASRANI aged 7

"Oh, now I can be seen, Mr Black will surely take me away!" said Mr Swing.

"Oh no, he won't," said Joe, and told Mr Swing all about the plans for making him as good as new.

"Hello," said a voice, and everyone turned to see Mr Black.

"Are you ready for your spring clean, Mr Swing?" I have driven the truck over and it is ready for you to be taken to the factory, to be repaired."

Joe watched, as Mr Black took a spanner and started to take the swing

to pieces. He did not see the Fairy and Fairy queen watching him, because grownups cannot see fairies very easily.

Joe turned to them, and said, "Thank you for looking after Mr Swing. I'm sure everything will be all right now."

"Goodbye, Joe," they said, and disappeared.

Joe walked home, just in time for tea.

The next day there was a letter for him; it was an invitation to a garden party at the park, on Sunday next.

"May I go please?" Joe asked his Mummy and Daddy.

"Of course you can," they both agreed.

On Sunday, Joe walked to the park.

In a corner of the park near to the playground, a long table had been set up with loads of sandwiches and cakes and drinks, and the in the middle of the playground was Mr Swing, beautifully painted in shiny bright colours.

"How smart you look!" said Joe.

"Oh, thank you Joe," said Mr Swing, as a little girl sat on his seat and started to swing backwards and forwards.

Joe walked to the table where all the food was and said hello to Mrs Green who was back from her holiday and sitting with Mr Black.

"Have some chocolate cake, Joe," they both said and Joe tucked in.

And they all lived happily ever after.

I would like to express my sincere thanks to all the schools, the Children, their parents and of course the teachers who undertook the daunting task of illustrating these stories. The scheme proved a resounding success and words cannot adequately express how impressed I was with all of the participants. Unfortunately, there was not enough room to include all the paintings and drawings received or was it possible to print them in colour.

My thanks go to Alexandra Harris for all her hard work in collating the information for this book and Robert Harris for his help with the editing. Any mistakes are entirely my own.

Thanks also to Charlotte Terry and Geraldine Baverstock and the Thames Team of Author House for helping to bring this book to print.

Brian Harris

The Children and schools who took part in illustrating this book
(listed in alphabetical order)

Alban Wood Primary School
The Brow, Watford, Hertfordshire, WD25 7NX
Leila Ali, aged 10
Basit Amadu, aged 9
Kelly Asojo, aged 9
Kelsey Ausden-Oliver aged 8
Syed Aziz, aged 10
Gage Barnett, aged 9
Troy Barrell-Cabey aged 10
Kyara Bentley, aged 9
James Blyth, aged 9
Ryan Brooks, aged 9
Nathan Broome, aged 9
Shaza Bukhari, aged 10
Ryan Chin, aged 9
Cavan Collins, aged 8
Kathleen Craig, aged 9
Alice Cripps, aged 9
Maegan Dibsdale-Hatch, aged 9
Alisha East, aged 9
Taylor Fernando, aged 9
Charlie Fisher, aged 9
Mia Ford, aged 8
Jordan Fraher, aged 9
Connie Gibson, aged 8
Lacey Gibson, aged 8
Ben Girvan, aged 10
Kieran Gower, aged 9
Elon Grant, aged 9
Joe Hailey, aged 8
Dipali Halai, aged 9
Charlie Hardwick, aged 9
Romanie Howell, aged 9
Emily Humphrey, aged 8
Olivia King, aged 9

Conor Knight, aged 9
Rebecca Long, aged 8
Kristal Manoochehri, aged 9
Sasha McGuigan, aged 9
Ross McKendrick, aged 10
Rosie Mejuto, aged 9
Nicole Murphy, aged 9
Ellie Nurse, aged 9
Kara O'Connell, aged 9
Lewis O'Shaughnessy, aged 9
Courtney Palmer, aged 8
Rhyanna Peters, aged 9
Mitchell Pooley, aged 8
Maria Razzag, aged 9
Sabah Razzaq, aged 9
Kaia Savino, aged 9
Aimee Shanahan, aged 8
Tyler Stanger, aged 10
Danny Stanger, aged 8
Gemmer Stanger, aged 9
Amy Steele, aged 10
Bethany Steer, aged 9
Michelle Tudorache, aged 8
Danielle Tuersley, aged 9
Cameron Walker, aged 10
Kye Welch, aged 8
Kia-Maria Whittaker, aged 9
Callum Wickes, aged 10
Lily Wilson, aged 9
Harriet Woods, aged 10
Ami Woodward, aged 8

Albury Church of England School
Church End, Albury, Hertfordshire, SG11 2JQ
Bethany Abery, aged 8
Jordan Badman, aged 8
Jessica Boodhun, aged 8
Zara Braceday, aged 7

Belinda Carini-Nunn, aged 10
Aydan Doyle, aged 10
Elanore Ewin, aged 8
Saira Fenton, aged 10
Jack Hancox, aged 7
Josh Reeves-Morris, aged 10
Sarah Townsley, aged 9
Lewis Trow, aged 8
Mia Welsh, aged 7
Maddie Wright, aged 11
Isabelle Wright, aged 7

Bushey Manor Junior School
Grange Road, Watford, Hertfordshire, WD23 2QL
Xavier Amachi, aged 7
Charlie Armitage, aged 10
Ella Bailey, aged 9
Joseph Baker, aged 7
Sean Barrett, aged 10
Leila Ben Yaklef, aged 9
Grace Ben-Nathan, aged 9
Simeon Ben-Nathan, aged 7
Oliver Benreniste, aged 9
Imogen Bernays, aged 8
Tehya Binham Thaker, aged 8
Hetty Bostock, aged 9
Gianna Buckridge, aged 7
Joanna Buckridge, aged 7
Oliver Castle, aged 8
Harry Chandler, aged 9
Alexander Clarke, aged 7
Cameron Clarke, aged 8
Harry Clements, aged 8
Max Jae Comissiong, aged 10
James Creavin, aged 9
Molly Culverhouse, aged 7
John Dakin, aged 7
Luka Delic, aged 7

Natash Deveraj, aged 7
Alfie Dibble, aged 9
Jack Doyle, aged 7
Rohan Dronsfield, aged 9
Rumor Phoenix Duffy, aged 10
Reggie Eldridge, aged 8
Louise Elson, aged 9
Alborz Fard, aged 8
Ross Filer, aged 8
George Forrester, aged 9
Brandon Fowler, aged 7
Rhys French, aged 7
Kian Garvey, aged 7
Cameron Ghai, aged 8
Sam Gray-Lisk, aged 10
Archier Green-Osobu, aged 8
Harrison Grinter, aged 8
Imogen Hadland, aged 7
Ella Hale, aged 9
Nairia Heath, aged 7
Elise Hefferman, aged 8
Duncan Henley-Washford, aged 7
Ryan Hewett, aged 9
Serena Hislop, aged 9
Elizabeth Holland, aged 9
Anthony Hope-Doherty, aged 10
Alyssa-Jade Horton, aged 10
Michael Houbart, aged 10
Jamie Howey, aged 8
Katy Rose Hoyles, aged 9
Amina Imansoura, aged 9
Sarah Imansoura, aged 8
Michael Jalpota, aged 8
Ag ne Joceryte, aged 8
Dean Johal, aged 10
Byron Johal, aged 8
Hannah Joint, aged 7
Saskia Jurascheck, aged 9

Ala Kalinska, aged 8
Antony Kavanagh, aged 8
Chloe Lawrence, aged 10
Abigail Layman, aged 10
Nicole Layman, aged 7
Joe Learmonth, aged 9
Oliver Leeks, aged 9
Connor Lowden, aged 7
Regan Mackenzie, aged 7
Jaya Mairs, aged 8
Robbie Marsh, aged 7
Felise Martin, aged 10
Harry Martin, aged 7
Ella May Marwood, aged 10
Jessica Marwood, aged 8
James Mascall, aged 10
Rayona Masrani, aged 7
Richard McCarthy, aged 10
Poppy McCarthy, aged 9
Kayleigh Millar, aged 9
Rohit Mitra, aged 9
Madison Moller, aged 9
Kai Morris, aged 10
Ananya Mudera, aged 9
Millie Murphy, aged 8
Danielle Nembhard, aged 10
Abigail O'Reilly, aged 7
Rhys O'Reilly aged 9
Mitchell Luke Palmer, aged 10
William Pardoe, aged 9
Lauren Parfitt, aged 7
Daisy Parker, aged 7
Fred Parker, aged 8
Mohina Patel, aged 8
Sam Probert, aged 8
Akshit Rana, aged 10
Jake Rasmussen, aged 9
Clare Reynolds, aged 8

Bailey Richards, aged 8
Jessica Rosewarn, aged 7
William Rutt, aged 7
Katie Schofield, aged 7
Lee Sharp, aged 9
Tommy Sharp, aged 8
Will Sheils, aged 9
Kate Sherwood, aged 9
Nathan Shugnell, aged 7
Alex Simmonds, aged 8
Umang Singh, aged 8
Emily A Smith, aged 10
James South, aged 9
Mia Springer, aged 9
Harvery Stephenson, aged 9
Ellis Stewart, aged 8
Annalise Stockley, aged 7
Maikanki Sutherson, aged 11
Myrhili Sutharson, aged 11
Jake Swaine, aged 10
Patrick Thomson, aged 7
Alexander Thomson, aged 9
Harry Tubbritt, aged 10
Elise Voyce, aged 9
Eleonora Vulpe, aged 10
Hannah Wales, aged 9
Bryn Walker, aged 9
Freya Walker, aged 7
Alex Walsh, aged 9
Alex Ward, aged 9
Daisy Wardell, aged 8
Chloe Watkins, aged 9
Harry Webster, aged 8
Isaac White, aged 9
Emily Whitehead, aged 7
Aaron Wilson, aged 7
Hewan Zewdu, aged 8

Clore Shalom School

Hugo Gryn Way, Shenley, Radlett, Hertfordshire, WD7 9BL

Joey Abels, aged 11

Sadie-Mae Arellano, aged 11

Emma Aroesti, aged 10

Aimee Bartman, aged 8

Liv Baxter, aged 8

Jamie Belasco, aged 8

Talia Bensoor, aged 10

Sasha Bensoor, aged 8

Hannah Rose Berger, aged 7

Robin Bernard, aged 10

Jack Bernstein, aged 10

Fiona Bowman, aged 8

Chiara Brown, aged 9

Joshua Burns, aged 8

Jordan Cannon, aged 10

Anna Chapman, aged 9

Hannah Cook, aged 9

Nathan Davis, aged 9

Jake Dousie, aged 10

Lily Elleswei, aged 8

Lorella Fifer, aged 7

Ben Franks, aged 8

Charlotte Garcia, aged 9

Henry Garnett, aged 8

Laura Gerber, aged 8

Ethan Gold, aged 9

Katie Goldlaing, aged 10

Ben Good, aged 8

Elie Harris, aged 8

Lia Hart, aged 8

Benjamin Heath, aged 7

Francesca Heath, aged 10

Matthew Helman, aged 11

Ellie Herman, aged 10

May Hyams, aged 11

Ela Karbaron, aged 9

Alexander Karpel, aged 9
Annie Kaye, aged 10
Zak Keizner, aged 9
Bethany Kinchuck, aged 7
Sasha Kirby, aged 8
Jake Kramer, aged 7
Ben Kushner, aged 8
James Lancer, aged 8
Thomas Lee, aged 10
Harrison Leighton, aged 8
Carli Levene, aged 7
Joel Levitan, aged 8
Jamie Linton, aged 11
Oliver Linton aged 7
Esther Liubarski, aged 7
Georgia Marcus, aged 10
Adam Marks, aged 8
Lauren McGurk, aged 8
Oliver Mendelsohn, aged 8
Abbi Minot, aged 8
Anouska Moss, aged 9
Ben Newington, aged 8
Joshua Newington, aged 11
Mikaela Noy, aged 7
Jake Posner, aged 11
Ameleah Press, aged 9
Andrea Prodromou, aged 11
Ellis Prodromou, aged 7
Benji Radnor, aged 8
Joseph Reissner, aged 8
Macy Richards, aged 9
Tia Richards, aged 10
Olivia Robinson, aged 9
Harley Rosen, aged 11
Amelia Rubens, aged 8
Alice Salem, aged 10
Aron Schechter, aged 7
Miles Schechter, aged 11

Laura Schuz, aged 11
Ma-ayan Schwartz, aged 10
Yuval Schwartz, aged 8
Lior Sharon, aged 9
Stephanie Sharon, aged 10
Jessica Shaw-Flynn, aged 7
Devon Shoob, aged 9
Jackson Shoob, aged 7
Robert Shurmer, aged 8
Alex Silverman, aged 7
Rebecca Skillman, aged 11
Liv Spalter, aged 9
Hannah Stead, aged 10
Rachel Stead, aged 8
Adam Steinberg, aged 11
Max Steinberg, aged 11
Danielle Stern, aged 12
Joshua Stern, aged 10
Kaylie Sunshine, aged 7
Teo Ungar, aged 8
Gavin Vaughan, aged 10
Mitchell Vaughan, aged 10
Hannah Wagman, aged 10
Karli Weinstein, aged 11
Melody White, aged 9
Jolyon Winkler, aged 10
Gemma Wise, aged 11
Harry Woolstone, aged 8
Leann Yfrah, aged 7
Jonah Zur, aged 9

Roebuck Primary School
St Margaret's, Stevenage, Hertfordshire, SG2 8RG
Chyna-Afrika Abbey, aged 7
Tiga-Ebony Abby, aged 10
Amy Ailey, aged 9
Lisa Ailey, aged 10
Olivia Allardyce, aged 9

Jonathan Ansell, aged 7
Manav Babbar, aged 9
Cameron Barker, aged 10
Charlotte Barnes, aged 8
Joshua Barnes, aged 10
Reece Bayford, aged 8
Marcus Bennett, aged 8
Rosie Borcherds, aged 10
Calum Briars, aged 10
Andrew Briffitt, aged 9
Chloe Brown, aged 10
Lauren Burrell, aged 7
Danny Carter, aged 7
Tia Carter, aged 10
Mollie Catlin, aged 10
Patrycia Ciosek, aged 9
Chelsea Cogdell, aged 9
Mason Corley, aged 9
Euan Cowan, aged 8
Lucy Dartnall, aged 7
Chloe Deamer, aged 8
Ben Drew, aged 10
George Drew, aged 8
Connor Elwood, aged 7
Jordan Emmerson, aged 10
Melissa Feltham, aged 10
Laura Flynn, aged 10
Lucy French, aged 7
Summer George, aged 10
Yousaf Ghulam, aged 7
Piotr Hajewski, aged 8
Ethan Hann, aged 9
Kessia Harris, aged 8
Jakeb Hart, aged 7
Kevin Hazime, aged 10
Christopher Hort, aged 7
Emily Johnson, aged 8
Hannah Jones, aged 8

Olivia Josland, aged 7
Lucy-May Kelleher, aged 7
Harry King, aged 7
Martin Kurek, aged 7
Matthew Lee, aged 9
Jared Lewis, aged 8
Ellie MacKenzie, aged 10
Bethany Maddox, aged 7
Abbie Madgin, aged 9
Lewis Marshall, aged 9
Promise Mboho, aged 7
Joe McGregor, aged 8
Megan Montgomery, aged 8
Hussam Mughal, aged 8
Jordan Nash, aged 10
Keziah Parnell, aged 7
Tayla Parnell, aged 7
Joe Petts, aged 9
Harrison Pinner, aged 10
Katy Pollard, aged 8
Jacob Richardson, aged 9
Jamie Richardson, aged 9
Kia-Maria Robins, aged 8
Luke Ryder, aged 7
Aelisha Saunders, aged 10
Owen Scales, aged 10
Jake Scales, aged 7
Lewis Scales, aged 7
Kieran Setterfield, aged 8
Kaleb Shaw, aged 8
Kaygen Shipper, aged 9
Tilly Stacey, aged 8
Aaron Stott, aged 10
Megan Thompson, aged 9
Nathan Townsend, aged 10
Jake Turrell, aged 8
Daniel Vickers, aged 9
Kira Wennington, aged 7

Kieran Whelan, aged 9
Shannon Whelan, aged 7
Janie Williamson, aged 9
Chloe Wilson, aged 9
Tommy Woods, aged 10
Katie Woolford, aged 10
Tasha Yeend, aged 7

Trotts Hill Primary School and Nursery
Wisden Road, Stevenage, Hertfordshire, SG1 5JD
Nadine Atkins, aged 8
Joshua Baker, aged 11
Bethany Bannister, aged 8
Connor Barrow, aged 10
Gina Beaven, aged 8
Dulcie Bell, aged 9
Paige Bentley, aged 11
Grace Boronte, aged 10
Chisembele Bwayla, aged 11
Natasha Bwalya, aged 11
Amy Cheriton, aged 10
Emilee Cleaver, aged 10
Jamie Clements, aged 9
Ashley Clynes, aged 8
Robyne Cooper-Tully, aged 10
Kieran Davis, aged 10
James Farbrother, aged 11
James Ferrari, aged 11
Drew Fisher, aged 11
Ben Gray, aged 9
Sophie Gray, aged 8
Jessica Hayes, aged 8
Chloe Hebbs, aged 10
Andrew Hunt, aged 9
Daniel Jones, aged 10
Millie Kay, aged 9
Katie Lewis, aged 10
Jack Morgan, aged 8

Harry Newberry, aged 11
Jasdeep Panesar, aged 10
Ellie Riley, aged 9
Joseph Simpson, aged 8

Whitehill Junior School
Whitehill Road, Hitchin, Hertfordshire, SG4 9HT
Jamie Addison, aged 7
Oskar Bogacki, aged 7
Callum Craig, aged 9
Daniel Davies-Gomez, aged 8
Samuel Hurley, aged 10
James Liu, aged 8
Adam Mountney, aged 8
Shannon O'Callaghan, aged 10
Marion Prud'hon, aged 8
Bradley Roberts, aged 11
Lily Sewell, aged 8
Elliot Thomas, aged 7
Alyssa Yap-Young, aged 8
Caitlin Yap-Young, aged 10
Dylan Yeupiksang, aged 7

Wymondley Junior School
Siccut Road, Little Wymondley, Hitchin, Hertfordshire, SG4 7HN
Rebekah Bacon, aged 10
Aime Ball, aged 9
Jeremy Beard, aged 10
Jose Burnigham, aged 10
Sam Challis, aged 9
Harry Cruttenden, aged 10
Jake Ebhodaghe, aged 9
Maitiu Emson, aged 10
Ryan Hart, aged 10
Emma Louise Watts, aged 10
Ellie Mann, aged 10
Paddy Marsh, aged 10
Georgie Marvell, aged 9

Fraser McGown, aged 10
Lowell Metcalfe, aged 10
Charlie Middleton, aged 9
Pavan Rai, aged 9
Emily Saunders, aged 9
Lucy Shaw, aged 10
Liam Sterling, aged 10
Ben Taylor, aged 10
Rachel Taylor, aged 9
Michaela Terry, aged 9
Aylish Toomey, aged 10
Samantha Walsh, aged 10
Matthew Williams, aged 10